HERE

is where we meet

HERE

is where we meet

JOHN BERGER

BLOOMSBURY

First published in Great Britain in 2005

Copyright © 2005 by John Berger

The moral right of the author has been asserted

Bloomsbury Publishing Plc, 38 Soho Square, London W1D 3HB

A CIP catalogue record for this book
is available from the British Library

ISBN 0 7475 7317 4

10 9 8 7 6 5 4 3 2 1

Typeset by Hewer Text Ltd, Edinburgh
Printed in Great Britain by Clays Ltd, St Ives plc

All papers used by Bloomsbury Publishing are natural,
recyclable products made from wood grown in well-managed
forests. The manufacturing processes conform to the
environmental regulations of the country of origin

For

Chloe
Lucy
Dimitri
Melina

Olek and
Maciek

Contents

I

Lisboa

In the centre of a square in Lisboa there is a tree called a Lusitanian (which is to say, Portuguese) cypress. Its branches, instead of pointing up to the sky, have been trained to grow outwards, horizontally, so that they form a gigantic, impenetrable, very low umbrella with a diameter of twenty metres. One hundred people could easily shelter under it. The branches are supported by metal props, arranged in circles around the twisted massive trunk; the tree is at least two hundred years old. Beside it stands a formal notice-board with a poem to passers-by written on it.

I paused to try to decipher a few lines:

> . . . I am the handle of your hoe, the gate of your house, the wood of your cradle and the wood of your coffin . . .

Elsewhere in the square chickens were pecking for worms on the unkempt grass. At several tables men were playing *sueca*, each one selecting and then placing his card on the table with an expression that combined wisdom and resignation. Winning here was a quiet pleasure.

It was hot – perhaps 28° C – at the end of the month of May. In a week or two, Africa, which begins – in a manner of speaking – on the far bank of the Tagus, would begin to impose a distant yet tangible presence. An old woman with an umbrella was sitting very still on one of the park benches. She had the kind of stillness that draws attention to itself. Sitting there on the park bench, she was determined to be noticed. A man with a suitcase walked through the square with the air of going to a rendezvous he kept every day. Afterwards a woman carrying a little dog in her arms – both of them looking sad – passed, heading down towards the Avenida da Liberdade. The old woman on the bench persisted in her demonstrative stillness. To whom was it addressed?

Abruptly, as I was asking myself this question, she got to her feet, turned and, using her umbrella like a walking stick, came towards me.

I recognised her walk, long before I could see her face. The walk of somebody already looking forward to arriving and sitting down. It was my mother.

It happens sometimes in my dreams that I have to phone my parents' flat, in order to tell them – or to ask them to tell somebody else – that I'm likely to be late, because I've missed a connection. I want to warn them that I'm not, at that moment, where I'm meant to be. The details vary from dream to dream, but the gist of what I have to tell them remains the same. What also remains the same is that I don't have my address book with me, and, although I attempt to remember their telephone number and try out several, I never find the right one. This corresponds with the truth that in my waking life I have forgotten the telephone number of the flat in which my parents lived for twenty years and which I once knew by heart. What, however, I forget in my dreams is that they are dead. My father died twenty-five years ago and my mother ten years later.

In the square, she took my arm and by common consent we crossed the street and walked slowly towards the top of the Mãe d'Agua staircase.

There's something, John, you shouldn't forget – you forget too much. The thing you should know is this: the dead don't stay where they are buried.

As she began talking, she didn't look at me. She looked concentratedly at the ground a few metres ahead of us. She was worried about tripping.

I'm not talking about heaven. Heaven is all very well, but I happen to be talking about something different!

She paused and chewed as if one of the words had

3

gristle on it and needed more chewing before being swallowed. Then she went on:

The dead when they're dead can choose where they want to live on Earth, always supposing they decide to stay on the Earth.

You mean they come back to some place where they were happy when they were alive?

We were by now at the top of the stairway and with her left hand she took hold of the rail.

You think you know the answers, you always did. You should have listened more to your father.

He had answers to many things. I see that today.

We took three steps down.

Your dear father was a man full of doubts, that's why I had to be behind him all the while.

To rub his back?

Amongst other things, yes.

Another four steps. She took her hand off the rail.

How do the dead choose where they want to stay?

She didn't answer, instead she gathered up her skirt and sat down on the next step of the staircase.

I've chosen Lisboa! she said, as if repeating something very obvious.

Did you ever come here – I hesitated, for I didn't want to make the distinction too blatant – *before*?

Again she ignored the question. If you want to find out something I didn't tell you, she said, or something you've forgotten, this is the time and place to ask me.

4

You told me so little, I observed.

Anybody can tell! Tell! Tell! I did something else. She looked demonstratively into the distance, towards Africa on the other side of the Tagus. No, I was never here before. I did something else, I showed you.

Is Father here?

She shook her head.

Where is he?

I don't know and I don't ask him. I fancy he may be in Rome.

Because of the Holy See?

For the first time she looked at me, the little triumph of a joke in her eyes.

Not at all; because of the tablecloths!

I put my arm round her. Gently, she removed my hand from her arm, and still holding it in hers, placed both our hands on the stone step.

How long have you been in Lisboa?

Don't you remember my warning you how it would be like this? I told you it would be like this. Beyond days or months or hundreds of years, beyond time.

Again she was peering towards Africa.

So time doesn't count, and place does? I said this to tease her. When I was a man, I liked teasing her and she went along with it, consenting, for it reminded us both of a sadness that had passed.

When I was a child her sureness enraged me (regardless of the argument involved). It was a sureness that revealed – at least to my eyes – how, behind the bravado, she was vulnerable and hesitant, whereas I wanted her to be invincible. Consequently, I would contradict whatever it was she was being so certain about, in the hope that we might discover something else, which we could question together with a shared confidence. Yet what happened, in fact, was that my counter-attacks made her more frail than she usually was, and the two of us would be drawn, helpless, into a maelstrom of perdition and lamentation, silently crying out for an angel to come and save us. On no occasion did an angel come.

The animals at least are here to help us, she said, looking at what she took to be a cat basking in the sun ten steps down.

It's not a cat, I said. It's an old fur hat, a chapka.

That's why I was a vegetarian, she said.

You loved fish! I contested.

Fish are cold-blooded.

What difference does that make? If it's a principle, it's a principle.

Everything in life, John, is a question of drawing a line, and you have to decide for yourself where to draw it. You can't draw it for others. You can try, of course, but it doesn't work. People obeying rules laid down by somebody else is not the same thing as respecting life. And if you want to respect life, you have to draw a line.

So time doesn't count and place does? I asked again.

It's not any place, John, it's a meeting place. There aren't many cities left with trams, are there? Here you can hear them all the while – except for a few hours during the night.

Do you sleep badly?

There's hardly a street in the centre of Lisboa where you can't hear trams.

It was a number 194, wasn't it? We took it every Wednesday from East to South Croydon and back. First we shopped in Surrey Street market, then we went to the Davies Picture Palace, with the electric organ that changed colour when the man played it. The number was 194, no?

I knew the organist, she said, and I bought celery for him in the market.

You also bought kidneys, despite being a vegetarian.

Your father enjoyed them for breakfast.

Like Leopold Bloom.

Don't show off! There's nobody here to notice. You always wanted to sit in the front of the tram, upstairs. Yes, it was a 194.

And climbing up the stairs you complained: Ah my legs, my poor legs!

You wanted to be up there in front because there you could drive and you wanted me to watch you drive.

I loved the corners!

7

The rails are the same here in Lisboa, John.

Do you remember the sparks?

In the damned rain, yes.

Driving after the cinema was best.

I never saw anyone look as hard as you did, sitting on the edge of your seat.

In the tram?

In the tram and in the cinema too.

You often cried in the cinema, I told her. You had a way of dabbing at your eyes.

The way you drove the tram pretty soon put a stop to that!

No, you really cried, most weeks.

Shall I tell you something? I don't suppose you've noticed the tower of Santa Justa, just down there? It's owned by the Lisboa Tramway Company. There's a lift in it and the lift goes nowhere really. It takes people up, they take a look around from the platform and then it brings them down again. Owned by the tramway company. Now, a film, John, can do the same thing. It takes you up and brings you back to the same place. That's one of the reasons why people cry in the cinema.

I'd have thought—

Don't think! There are as many reasons for crying in the cinema as there are people who buy tickets.

She licked her lower lip, a gesture she also used after applying lipstick. On one of the roofs above the Mãe d'Agua staircase a woman was singing as she pegged out

8

sheets on a line to dry. Her voice was plaintive and the sheets were very white.

When I first came to Lisboa, my mother said, I came down in that lift of the Santa Justa. I have never been up in it – you understand? I came down in it. Like we all do. That's why it was built. It's lined with wood like a first-class railway carriage. I've seen a hundred of us in it. It was built for us.

It only takes about forty, I said.

We weigh nothing. And do you know the first thing I saw, when I stepped out of the lift? A shop for digital cameras!

She got to her feet and started climbing back up the staircase. She had a certain difficulty in breathing, and so, to make it easier, to encourage herself, she blew out in long hisses between her lips, pursed as if for whistling. It was she who first taught me to whistle. We at last reached the top.

For the moment I am not leaving Lisboa, she said. For the moment I'm waiting.

Whereupon she turned round and made for the bench she had been sitting on, and the square became demonstrably still, so still that she eventually vanished.

During the next few days she kept herself hidden. I wandered around the city, watching, drawing, reading, talking. I wasn't looking for her. From time to time, however, I was reminded of her – usually by something only half-seen.

Lisboa is a city which has a relationship with the visible world like no other city. It plays a game. Its squares and streets are paved with patterns of white and coloured stones, as if, instead of being roads, they were ceilings. Its walls, both indoors and outdoors, are covered with the famous *azulejos* tiles wherever you look. And these tiles speak of the fabulous things to be seen in the world: a monkey playing pipes, a woman picking grapes, saints praying, whales in the ocean, crusaders in their boats, basilica plants, magpies in flight, lovers embracing, a tame lion, a Moreia fish with spots like a leopard. The tiles of the city draw attention to the visible, to what can be seen.

At the same time these same decorations on walls and floors, around windows and down staircases, are saying something different, in fact the opposite. Their crackly white ceramic surfaces, their vivacious colours, the mortar joints around them, the repeated patterns, all insist upon the fact that they are covering something up, and that whatever is behind them or beneath them, will remain, thanks to them, invisible and hidden for ever!

As I walked I saw the tiles as if they were playing cards which hid more of the game than they revealed. I walked and climbed and turned between deal after deal, hand after hand, and I remembered her playing patience.

Nobody seems to agree about the number of hills on

which the city is built. Some say seven, like Rome. Others dispute this. Whatever the number may be, the city centre is built on steep, precipitous, rocky ground rising and falling every few hundred metres. And for centuries its steep streets have appropriated every device imaginable to banish vertigo: steps, enclaves, landings, impasses, curtains of washing, windows at floor level, little yards, railings, shutters; everything is used to offer shelter from the sun and the winds, and to blur any distinction between indoors and outdoors.

Nothing could induce her to go closer than fifty metres to a cliff-edge.

Between the stairways and the belvederes and the washing in the Alfama district, I got myself lost several times.

Once we were trying to get out of London and had taken the wrong road. Father stopped the car and unfolded a map. We are going far, far, too far to the west, Mother said. I have a good bump for direction, a phrenologist told me so more than once. He could feel it here. She was touching the back of her head. She had very fine hair with which she was never comfortable. He said my bump for places was here.

Nobody, I retorted from the back seat, takes phrenology seriously any more. They were a bunch of crypto-fascists.

Why do you say that?

You can't measure a person's gifts with a pair of calipers. And anyway, where did they get their norms from? From the Greeks, of course. Narrowly European. Racist.

The one who felt my head was Chinese, she muttered.

They divided people into just two categories, I said, pure and degenerate!

They were right about me anyway! I have a good bump for places! We've come too far, we should have turned left miles back, where we saw that poor man without any legs. Now we may as well go on – no point in turning back, it's too late. If we can, we should take the next on the left.

It's too late! was one of her favourite phrases. And hearing it, I was invariably filled with fury. Some event, trivial or grave, would have prompted her to use it. Yet the phrase seemed to me to refer not to an event, but to the way time folds – something I began noticing from about the age of four – the folds ensuring that some things can be saved and others cannot. She would pronounce the three words lightly, without pathos, almost as if she was quoting a price. And my fury was partly against this calm. Maybe it was the example of her calm, combined with my fury, which later made me study History.

I thought of this while I drank a small cup of sharp coffee in an Alfama bar, the size of a caravan. I looked at the faces of the other men, all over fifty, weathered in the same way. Lisboetas often talk of a feeling, a mood, which they call *saudade*, usually translated as nostalgia, which is incorrect. Nostalgia implies a comfort, even an indolence such as Lisboa has never enjoyed. Vienna is the capital of nostalgia. This city is still, and has always been, buffeted by too many winds to be nostalgic.

Saudade, I decided as I drank a second coffee and watched a drunk's hands carefully arranging the accurate story he was telling as if it were a pile of envelopes, *saudade* was the feeling of fury at having to hear the words *too late* pronounced too calmly. And Fado is its unforgettable music. Perhaps Lisboa is a special stopover for the dead, perhaps here the dead show themselves off more than in any other city. The Italian writer Antonio Tabucchi, who loves Lisboa deeply, spent a whole day with the dead here.

The following Sunday I was in the Baixa district, crossing the immense Praça do Comércio. The Baixa is the only district of the old city that is flat and low. Surrounded on three sides by the famous hills, its fourth side is the estuary of the Tagus, known as the Sea of Straw because its waters, in a certain light, have a golden sheen. From the landing stages here during the fifteenth century, Lisboa's navigators, merchants and slave-traders set out for Africa, the Orient and, later, Brazil. Lisboa was then the richest capital of Europe, trading in everything which defied the

Atlantic: gold, slaves from the Congo, silks, diamonds, spices.

Stick two cloves into each apple, she'd instruct, and then we'll bake them in the oven with brown sugar.

When she wasn't looking I'd stick in a third, with the conviction that this would make the apple taste finer.

If she spotted the third one, she'd take it out and put it back in the jar. They come from Madagascar, she explained. Waste not, want not!

This was another phrase of hers that was like a refrain. Yet unlike It's Too Late, Waste Not, Want Not was a warning rather than a lament. A warning which somehow applied, I thought as I walked across it, to the Praça do Comércio. All its dimensions with their projected geometries are those of an unrealisable dream.

A fatal earthquake, the tidal waves that accompanied it, the fires that followed it, devastated a third of Lisboa and killed tens of thousands of its inhabitants during the first week of November 1755. Famine, disease and looting ensued. While the fires were still burning, and people had only the tattered clothes they stood up in, men bought and sold looted diamonds among ashes and rubble. Despite the blue sky above, despite the golden tan of the Sea of Straw, there was talk everywhere of Punishment and Retribution.

And it was the following year that the Marquês de Pombal began to dream of a new city of Reason and Symmetry. After a catastrophe that had shaken the optimism and sense of justice of philosophers the length

14

of Europe, the rebuilt city of Lisboa was going to propose a prosperity, a security guaranteed by the flow of wealth alone! A banker's dream of streets whose regularity, transparency, parallel lines and reliability would match those of perfectly kept accounts, and whose immense Praça do Comércio would open the city to the trade of the entire world . . .

Yet in the second half of the eighteenth century Lisboa was neither Manchester nor Birmingham, and the Industrial Revolution had started elsewhere. The decline that would lead to Portugal becoming the poorest nation in Western Europe had already set in.

However many people there are in the Praça do Comércio, it always looks half-empty.

She kept little in her purse. Her movements, when handling cash, were neat and precise. She hid small sums that she had ear-marked for certain projects in different envelopes, or in the drawers of her dressing table, so she wouldn't be tempted to spend them. Once she lost a ten-shilling note, which represented a third of a working woman's monthly wage. It's gone! she sobbed. It's gone! She said this as if the note had chosen to go, as if it were an animal who had run away, ungratefully run away, for she was giving it a good home. Gone!

When she wept, she tried to turn away from me. This

may have been to spare me, but it was also because her tears took her back to other times, before I had been thought of. While she was crying, I waited, like you wait for a long train to pass at a level crossing.

After a while she dabbed her eyes and said: We'll manage. All we have to do is to make a little go a long way.

By now I was in the Rua Augusta, one of the straight streets of which the banker had dreamt. Being Sunday, the opticians and hairdressers, the travel agencies and maritime insurance offices were shut. People were on their way to have lunch with family or friends. Many were carrying little packages of sweetmeats to offer to their hosts; Sunday gifts, elaborately wrapped and tied with their ribbons knotted in bows.

On the corner of the Rua da Conceição a crowd waited on the pavement, peering towards the Madalena church. I decided to wait too. There was no traffic. Even the trams had been stopped.

I heard people cheering further down the street. Then 150 runners appeared, coming from the direction of the Madalena. They were running steadily, keeping together in a bunch, encouraging one another, with no bravura or overt competitiveness. Men and women, teenagers and seventy-year-olds, all with their heads held high, some snorting like horses when they breathed out. Their long strides beat out a slow regular rhythm on the cobbles between the tram lines.

A child, who wanted to see better, pushed me in the

back and I stepped a little to one side. Certain runners clenched their fists, others let them hang loose. The women seemed to keep their hands more or less at the same level as their hips, whereas with the men the hands were often higher up, level with their chests. The child who had pushed me in the back turned out to be her. She quickly took my hand. All her life she had cold hands.

Nobody in this half-marathon, she whispered, knows whether they'll make it to the end. And that's part of the secret, not to try! The magic number is seventeen. What they're all telling themselves now is: Make it to the seventeenth lap!

How many laps have they done?

Ten. This is the tenth. Seven more to go to seventeen. After the seventeenth, the last four laps – that's when the lower stomach is in danger of cramps – the last four look after themselves! You needn't worry about them, they're beyond you. See that man's face, see how his face is stretched by the effort he's making.

It's stretched into a kind of smile.

And the smile is acknowledging his own name!

What's his name?

Costa. Bravo, Costa!

And her?

Madalena!

You know all their names?

Madalena's face is stretched too. Madalena is smiling! Bravo, Madalena!

One man had Luiz written on his T-shirt. Luiz! I shouted, not to be out-done.

José and Dominique! she screamed.

Smiling every one! I said.

This is not a city, my boy, which fucks itself up. That's why I'm here.

I glanced at her. She too was smiling and there were so many creases around her eyes that her old woman's face looked like crumpled paper. Then she repeated: Not a city that fucks itself up, that's something I know.

Her voice had changed. It had become the voice of a seventeen-year-old. It had the somatic assurance, the impudence, of being that age. Such impudence begins with the tongue, quite apart from what it says or doesn't say, quite apart from being shy or brazen. The impudence of the tongue running with its tip along its own white teeth while saying nothing. Or, at a given unforeseeable moment, the impudence of its sudden proposal to enter and probe somebody else's mouth – boy's or girl's.

I glanced at her. It was a century ago since she was seventeen.

We walked in the direction of the Chiado and, suddenly, on the spur of the moment, I found myself entering a baker's to ask whether they had a dessert, a kind of custard flan with almonds called Bacon from Heaven. It's sweet, tastes like marzipan and has nothing to do with bacon. *Toicino do Céu*. My mother stayed outside. Yes, they do. I bought two portions and the baker's wife made a gift package with a ribbon, the colour of the Sea of Straw. I stepped out into the street.

It's what I like best. How on earth did you know? she asks me in her seventeen-year-old voice. Every afternoon I have a *Toicino do Céu*, she added.

We found a café near the Praça de Luiz de Camões, decorated with blue and white *azulejos*.

The blue on these tiles, she said, is the same as Reckitt's Blue. Every little square packet was wrapped in this blue.

I remember turning the wringer to wring the water out of the sheets for you.

After doing the wringing there was water everywhere. There were mops.

You helped a lot before you went to school.

Before I went to school nothing ever came to an end. Can you guess what the most fabulous object in my childhood was?

You sound like somebody writing an autobiography. Don't!

Don't what?

You're bound to get it wrong.

Do you want to guess what the most fabulous object in my childhood was?

Tell me.

Your barometer!

The one beside Father's desk? We took it with us whenever we moved. And Father got out his toolbox and screwed it to the wall. I forget how many times. Many, many times. It was a wedding present.

There's a metal plaque pinned to it which says so.

The Boy Scouts had that plaque engraved specially.

You were married on the sixth of February 1926 and I was born on the fifth of November the same year!

It doesn't say that! How could they know? Though I knew the very second you were conceived.

I must have been conceived on your wedding night in Paris. That would make exactly nine months!

I loved Paris. Ever since the first time, I've loved Paris.

I know.

The pillowcases and the statue of Molière!

Why aren't you there now, then? You could have chosen Paris.

You can't live a honeymoon all your life, can you?

No, Maman, but perhaps all your death!

This made her laugh until she had to dab her eyes. It was a silver laugh, like a small jet of water in a decorated urn in the Alhambra.

The barometer is still working, I said.

It was a good make. It'll last several lifetimes.

Every day you went up to look at it, and you tapped with your knuckles against the glass and you looked at it again and then you announced: It's going up! Or, the next day: It's coming down!

Have you ever seen a barometer that stays still?

Yes, in Africa.

We weren't in Africa, were we?

And do you know what I believed?

She laughed again, jutting her lower lip up towards her nose.

I watched you when you polished and dusted the barometer. Then you tapped it, not once, but three, four, five, six times, and I saw the secret smile on your face and I knew that you had changed what was going to happen! The needle would shift, the prophesy would be altered. It would be closer to FAIR, leaving CHANGE further behind. On other days, if you were anxious and hadn't received the letter you were waiting for, or didn't like the book from the public library you were reading, you tapped hard on the glass, and the needle shifted closer to STORMY. And it was never wrong. If it pointed to STORMY, stormy it would be.

So, you believed I was in control?

I did.

I kept a good many things under control, I had to.

Never me!

I never tried with you.

No?

People try to control whatever risks to get out of control, that's to say what has been controlled before. I left you alone from the beginning.

I felt alone.

To my great surprise, my boy, you were free.

I was scared by one thing after another. I still am.

Naturally. How could it be otherwise? You can either be fearless, or you can be free, you can't be both.

To know how to be both is surely the aim of all philosophy, Mother.

It's not philosophy that takes you there.

She started to nibble her favourite flan.

For a few moments love can, she added.

Were you there often?

Once or twice.

When she said this she smiled. The smile accompanying an unsaid password.

You know, don't you? I said, that after your funeral all of us learnt, to our considerable surprise, that you'd been married and divorced long before you met Father.

Everything comes out in the wash! she said. We loved each other a lot, the first husband and I.

So what made you get divorced?

Because I wanted to have children! She pointed at me with a finger that had custard on it. I didn't know what either of you would be like, but I wanted children.

And he didn't?

He and I looked at the stars together. And I wasn't in a hurry. I was only seventeen. To tell the truth, I was sixteen when I met him – 1909, the year I read Maeterlinck's *The Blue Bird*. I met him in the Tate Gallery where I was looking, as on every Sunday, at the Turner watercolours. He invited me to have a cup of tea – there wasn't much coffee in those days – and he told me all about Turner's double life as an old man. I thought *he* was an old man – though he was only half as old as you are today. And I remember wondering whether he had a double life too. The next Sunday he told me the story of Miriam.

You mean the Bible story?

He told me both. The Bible story and my story. And do you know something? He was the first person ever to call me Miriam! At home I'd always been Mim. I left the stables and the warehouse horses my father looked after and I was Mim. I walked across Vauxhall Bridge, and on the other side of the Thames where he greeted me, I was suddenly Miriam.

You married him when?

He'd come back from India, and I thought that if I married him, it would be a way of keeping him. I kept him for nine years; for nine years he was happy with his Miriam.

He didn't work?

He wondered about things, he asked questions. And I learnt and I read so I could talk with him. Sometimes we talked all night. He'd wake me up and take me out into the garden, we had a big garden, and at the bottom of it was a bust of Seneca, and nobody could see us and we'd stand there like Adam and Eve watching the sun come up.

Like Adam and Eve?

Naked.

The house was where?

Croydon.

Croydon! I shouted in surprise.

Shh! Don't shout, people will look at us; people don't

shout in this city. I still remember the words I learnt by heart sitting under that statue: 'You must want nothing, if you wish to challenge Jupiter who himself wants nothing!'

But by now you wanted children and Jupiter didn't!

Don't be vulgar. Alfred worshipped me. Do you understand? He made me feel very beautiful. Your father was a more manly man; Charles worshipped me from afar.

Did Father meet him?

After the divorce he left his house and became a tramp.

That must have been hard on you.

It was what he wanted.

You went on seeing him?

I see him still. Like I'm seeing you now.

He's here in Lisboa?

If ever a man should go straight to heaven, it would be Alfred. He was a saint. Saints are not easy to live with. But saint he was. He's not in Lisboa.

I think I saw him once.

You couldn't have!

One day in Croydon you left me in a big store.

Kennards!

You left me in Kennards' toy department.

You loved watching the trains. The new electric trains, not the clockwork.

You took me to the toy department and you said: Wait here, John, I won't be gone long. I waited. The trains seemed to go slower and slower. I wasn't worried, but it was a long while. I watched the signals change colour a thousand times. When you came back you looked very flushed, as if you'd been running. We took the lift straight down to the ground floor. Outside, behind the store, in a back street, a man stood on the pavement blocking our way, and you put your handkerchief up to your face. His clothes were held together with string. He had a straggling beard. And his expression! I couldn't take my eyes off his face.

Alfred! my mother whispered in the café with the blue and white *azulejos*.

He was twice as large as you, I said, and his decrepitude made him look larger still. You remember what happened next? He gave you something in a packet.

It was some letters. He said he didn't have any place to keep them now that he was on the street, and he couldn't bring himself to destroy them, so he wanted to give them back to me.

Do they still exist?

She shook her head.

I burnt them, burnt them as soon as we got home.

Then he put out a filthy hand and ruffled my hair and he said to you: He needs taking care of.

My mother started to cry in the café with the *azulejos*.

When something has to go, she sobbed, I don't hesitate.

You were still in love with him?

He had eyes that burnt through you, she murmured.

The moment I saw him I knew that wherever you had been that afternoon you'd been with him. And I told myself I would never tell anybody.

He died soon after. He was knocked down by a car that didn't stop. They thought he was a tramp.

She put her hands up to hide her face.

It's dangerous, she said, chewing on the words, to live just on virtue, or what Seneca called wisdom, even if it's true virtue, it's dangerous. It leads to addiction, like drink. I've seen it.

Why did he say I needed taking care of?

She lowered her hands.

He could tell by looking at you. You were ten, and you had a mouth that was always hanging open.

Did he know that you had children?

I hid nothing from him.

A face so full of pain, I said.

There followed a long silence during which we both looked out of the window and watched the white of the buildings outstaring the blue of the sky. Then she said: Alfred taught me and I taught you and I'm telling you that what you saw in his face wasn't only pain. Not only pain. I'm going to take a little rest now.

She got to her feet and walked slowly towards the toilets.

She is serving mashed potatoes. Nice and fluffy, she says, still stirring them with a fork. She wears a kerchief over her hair. She worked all day in the kitchen of the tea-house in which we lived. She suffered from the heat of the stoves, yet when she sucked her fingers because they had icing sugar or homemade custard on them, she couldn't help smiling: the sweetness folding into her pastry pride, for she knew she was a good cook. I see her writing in her diary. She bought herself one every year, often waiting until February when they were sold cheaper. The diaries she chose invariably had a small thin pencil attached to them. The pencil slipped through a loop and lay along the golden edges of the pages. Smaller and thinner than a cigarette – she smoked then a brand of cigarettes called Du Maurier – it was often the only pencil we could find to write something down with. Sometimes I drew with it. Be sure to give it back to me. It was always carefully reinserted into its loop. And with it she makes her diary entries, noting her rare appointments, and each day systematically, the weather. Morning: rain. Afternoon: bright patches.

The next time I saw her was on a bright morning.

The trams in the centre of Lisboa are very different from the red double-decker ones that used to run in Croydon; they are as cramped as small fishing boats and they are a lemon yellow. Their drivers, as they negotiate the steep one-way streets like straits, and nose their way round blind jetties, give the impression of hauling in ropes and holding rudders rather than turning wheels and operating levers. Yet despite the sudden descents, the lurches, the choppiness, the passengers, mostly elderly, remain contemplative and calm – as if they were still sitting in their living rooms or visiting a neighbour. And indeed, in places, the trams, with their open windows, sway so close to these rooms that it would be easy to reach out and touch a birdcage hanging from a balcony and with a little push set it swinging.

I had caught the number 28 going to the destination of Prazeres (Pleasures), which is the name of an old cemetery where the mausoleums have front doors with window panes through which you can look at the abodes of the departed. Many are furnished with low tables, a chair, bunks with bedspreads, rugs, photographs, statues of the Madonna, cushions. One has a pair of dancing shoes on a rug. Another has a bicycle and a fishing rod leaning against the wall facing the bunk with a small coffin on it.

I had got on the tram at the church in the district of Gracia, which is at the opposite end of the line from the cemetery, and it was when we were passing through the next district of Bairro Alto that I saw my mother again. Like other pedestrians in the narrow street, she was flattening herself against a shop-front to let the tram, which was ringing its bell, pass by. She spotted me notwithstanding and, at the next corner, where the tram stopped and its two sets of doors unfolded noisily like wooden curtains, she climbed aboard with a triumphant air, took a ticket out of her purse and, using the usual umbrella as a stick, came to stand beside me and slip her arm through mine. A dog sitting at the feet of another old woman wagged its tail, which thumped on the floor. The wooden curtains shut. The electro-motor whined to gather enough momentum for the tram to start. She said nothing, she simply handed me a plastic bag with the logo of the Colombo Shopping Centre printed on it.

At the next stop, when the wooden curtains opened again, she said: We're going to the market, I take it?

Yes, that was my idea.

On hearing me say Yes, she laughed her seventeen-year-old laugh.

We get off, she said, in one minute and and it's downhill all the way to the Mercado da Ribeira.

Seen from its interior, the Mercado da Ribeira resembles a pagoda, a pagoda constructed of carved stone, glass and metal. The engineering challenge must have been to find the best way of letting in daylight and, simultaneously, of offering shade from the punishing summer heat. The solution was to make it tall and only to let the light enter sideways.

There are surprisingly few flies, even where the raw meats are hanging. She leads me, tripping light-footedly, umbrella scarcely touching the flagstones, past the vegetables and fruit, to the avenues of fish.

It crosses my mind that the Mercado da Ribeira is why she chose to come to Lisboa.

Large fish markets are strange places because when you enter one, you enter another kingdom. The stony sea urchins, the locust lobsters, the lampreys, the squids, the lings, the turbots, insist that here the measures of time and space, of longevity and pain, of light and darkness, of alertness and sleepiness, of recognition and indifference are altered. For example, fish never stop growing; the older they are, the larger they are. A sixty-year-old sandy ray measuring two metres would, most of the time, live in what would seem to us total darkness. Fish can detect hormones by their smell in the water. They also have an additional sixth sense, which is that of their lateral line, a kind of elongated eyelid, running from gills to tail, sensitive to vibrations, sounds and sudden disturbances. There are 45,000 species of shellfish, all of them constituting food for others, all of them eaters. The age, relative immutability and cyclic complexity of this other kingdom is somewhat humbling.

They know me well here, my mother announces without a trace of humility.

She did not believe in humility. Humility was, in her opinion, a pretence, a tactic of diversion while the person involved covertly aimed at something else. Perhaps she was right.

Now she is bending over a basket of lady crabs. Their dark shells are like brown velvet, with a down on them so that they are as soft to touch as their nippers are sharp, and on their legs are smears of blue, as if they had sidled their way through oil.

The choicest of all crabs, she says. Here they call them *naralheira felpuda*. *Felpuda* means 'hairy'.

30

She straightens her back and looks into my eyes with an expression I've not seen before.

I've learnt a lot since my death. You should use me while you are here. You can look things up in a dead person like in a dictionary.

Her expression is one of happy impertinence, for she is sure now that she is beyond reach.

We walk down one of the aisles of the pagoda, past flounders, tunny fish, John Dories, mackerel, sardines, anchovies, sabre fish.

The sabre, she says, looking up at the distant roof, her little short nose in the air, the sabre only comes up from his depths to the surface at night when there's a full moon!

All the fishmongers are women. Women with strong shoulders, hefty forearms, wearing rubber boots, handling the ice as if it was hot metal, and their tied scarves and slightly mocking eyes are very feminine. They treat the fish they're selling as they might treat distant, mildly irritating, members of the family. Irritating because not as alert as they once were!

My mother picks up a grey shrimp to smell it. The vendor, who is gutting a fish, smiles at her.

Get half a pint, Mother says. Ask Andreas here, her name's Andreas, she has a husband in Cuba and a daughter who is an air hostess.

Andreas holds up the fish she is gutting and points very gently with the tip of her knife at what looks like a soft roe nestling near the top of the fish's emptied stomach cavity. Shiny, whitish-pink, curvy – like a foxglove just before it opens.

It's a whiting, Mother says.

The tip of the knife moves carefully down the stomach cavity and now touches an orange-coloured granular sack, the same orange and the same size as a dried apricot. Hard female roe.

Hermaphrodite! Andreas announces smiling, and then repeats: Hermaphrodite! as if she does not want us to get over our surprise. Hermaphrodite!

I pay for the shrimps and we proceed down the aisle, each of us eating them and throwing the heads and tails on the floor.

We walk down another aisle and we pass a slab on which there are a dozen of the reddest fish I've seen. Scarlet with a fire in their red such as no flower has, not even a tropical one.

Atlantic redfish, Mother murmurs. They too have strange mating habits. First of all, they're not mature until they are ten years old, which is very late. Next, the males fast for two months. Then they have intercourse, like animals do, with the sperm entering the female. She keeps it there for four months until all her eggs are ready, thirty, fifty or a hundred thousand. Then she lets the sperm fertilise them. After a while the eggs hatch into larvae inside her. And nine months after intercourse she lays the larvae deep in the Atlantic.

I've always put life before writing, I say.

Don't boast.

It's true.

Then pass over it in silence.

Supposing now I don't understand what I note down.

Others may.

We stop before a bank of salmon.

Salmon was Father's favourite dish, wasn't it?

Yes, she says, but since his death he prefers swordfish. The espadarte! The espadarte with its upper beak, which is like a blade, and long, long – a third of his whole length – and with the blade he slashes out left and right to kill the fishes he is hunting, each with a single blow. It was a swordfish – wasn't it? – that the old man of the sea wrestled with in Hemingway's story. The book made me think of your father and of life in the trenches during the Great War. What's the connection? you will ask. I can't explain everything. The story made me think of your father and the war. I can't explain why.

A connection of courage?

She nods.

I never saw a man who wept as often as your father and I never knew a man who was half as brave.

She nods her head again. I take her arm.

The strangest thing of all, John, is that the flesh of the espardarte – which must never be confused with the silver sabre fish – the flesh of this huge fish, when it is marinaded and cooked, is the most tender, the most delicate, and the whitest in the world. It dissolves in the mouth – you don't bite – it tastes like a soufflé. Each time, after I've cooked it, I place it on his plate like a kiss.

He comes to eat it here?

Of course not. He'll eat it, wherever he is, when he happens to think of me. Just as I think of him when I'm preparing it.

Do we have to find an espadarte, I ask, or can we just think of one like we're doing now?

What are you saying? I told you, it has to be marinated in lemon juice and olive oil! So we have to find lemons and a green pepper and a yellow pepper and a red one. You cut up the peppers and put them in the pan first so they give off their liquid, then you pop in the fish. A slice, weighing about 300 grams, not too thin, a thick slice taken from a juicy lateral cut from across the swordfish's belly. Takes very little time to cook – it must never be over-cooked – best to put a lid on the pan. Some serve it with capers, I don't. I'll get the fish, you go and find the lemon and peppers.

She didn't turn up again for several days. I took the ferry to Calilhas on the other side of the Tagus. Looking back across the water at Lisboa, each large building was recognisable, each district, as marked on the street map, could easily be distinguished and given its name, the hills behind seemed to have pushed the city nearer to the sea, to the sea's very edge, and strangest of all was the impression I had from this distance that Lisboa had removed all its clothes and was naked! I didn't know

34

whether this was due to shadows from the clouds, or to a refraction of sunlight coming off the Sea of Straw, or whether it was because I had entered the zone where, throughout centuries, sailors and fishermen had found again, or looked back at for the last time, the Lisboa they loved.

The next day the weather was gusty with squalls of Atlantic rain. I was crossing the Campo dos Mártires da Pátria with an anorak pulled over my head. The rain came in fits and starts and when it came, it was drenching. The martyrs of the fatherland, after whom the square is named, were executed here by hanging in 1817. The gallows stood where the roundabout now is. All twelve of them were Freemasons. The execution was ordered by Marshal Beresford, for at that time, after Wellington's Peninsular War, the English were governing the country. The twelve men were accused of being republicans and conspirators. As they were being blindfolded they prayed for the city.

And this square, with its roundabout and trams and unending traffic, is still strangely full of prayers. You edge your way between prayers, as between cattle in a livestock market. The martyrs' prayers. The prayers of those who are obliged to visit the city morgue, beside the Institute of Forensic Medicine to the north of the square, and the prayers of all those who come here to have the blessing of the man whose statue has been placed in the middle of the roundabout: Dr José Thomas de Souza Martins.

Around this statue stand stone tablets which look a little like headstones for graves. Some lean against the plinth of the statue, others against one another. In fact they are not tombstones: written on them are prayers of thanks to the doctor who once cured a cirrhosis, or a bronchitis, some haemorrhoids, a case of impotence, a child's asthma, a woman's stress, a colitis . . . Some of the cures were performed during his lifetime, some after his death.

Old women are selling photos of him in the square. Framed and unframed. Dr Martins looked somewhat like my Uncle Edgar – who was my father's elder brother, a man of learning who never stopped learning, a man of ideals who never despaired, a man whom everyone, including my mother, treated as a failure, a man with a wart on the middle finger of his right hand where he held his pen writing hundreds of pages of a book that nobody ever read or published.

What their two faces had in common was an unusual looseness about the mouth, indicating not weakness but a desire to kiss rather than to bite. They also had similar foreheads, foreheads not of imposing intelligence but of an immense, inspiring calm. Today, a century after his death, Dr Martins is referred to in Lisboa as Doctor of the Heavens and of the Earth. And my Uncle Edgar still demonstrates to me the power of reticent love.

The wind was smacking wet, and the gulls were flying very low over the roofs. It was a day when everyone turned their backs to the sea, if they had no one out on it.

Women, crouched under dark umbrellas in the middle of the roundabout, were selling candles. Three sizes of candles, priced accordingly, though no price was marked. The largest were thirty centimetres tall, their wax the colour of parchment. Nearer the statue of the doctor, lit candles were burning on two metal tables. The table-tops, encrusted with old melted wax, had spikes for impaling the new candles on, and a tall metal sheet behind to cut the wind. I watched the flames. They flickered, they guttered, they were blown sideways as if coming from a toy dragon's mouth; yet not one of them had succumbed to the rain or the gale-force wind. A man with a black hat and the face of a gypsy stood close by, surveying them with a protective air. Perhaps, when the wind veered, he shifted the tables or the metal sheets to protect the flames, and perhaps he asked for a little money from the candle-makers for this bad-weather job. Or was he simply standing there like me, fascinated by the tenacity of the flames?

Slowly the idea came to me to buy and light some candles myself. I knew who they would be for. I was thinking of three friends who at that moment, for different reasons, were at sea.

I bought the tallest candles, which would burn longest, and I walked over to one of the tables. I impaled them, one after the other, on the three nearest spikes. Only afterwards did it occur to me that I should first have lit one from a burning candle, then I could have lit my other two with it once they were impaled. Now it would be difficult in the wind to light them with a match, and anyway I didn't have any matches.

As I realised my mistake, a small woman from behind offered me a lit candle. I took it, without looking round, not doubting for a moment who it was! Then I stood there, mesmerised by the three new, flickering flames.

When I did at last turn round, I was amazed to discover that the small woman behind with an umbrella was not my mother.

I'm so sorry, sorry, I blurted out, I thought you were my mother! I spoke in French, which is the language I fall into when I'm confused.

I think I'm almost young enough to be your daughter, she replied lightly, speaking a French with a Portuguese accent. I gave her back her candle, which was still burning, and I bowed.

Once they are alight, she said, whatever good they may do, they do it without us.

Of course, I whispered, of course.

I saw you were at a bit of a loss, she said.

You speak French very well.

I worked in Paris. Cleaning. Last year I was fifty-five and I said to myself, it's time to come back to Lisboa for good. And my husband came too.

Can I offer you a coffee out of the rain?

No, I'll place my candle and I must get along home.

She had blue eyes in a face that was strong yet unprotected.

It's for my husband, mine.

He's ill?

No, he's not ill. He had an accident. Fell off the roof he was working on.

Is he badly hurt?

She stared at my chest as if it were the distant Sea of Straw. I knew then that he was dead.

You should have brought an umbrella like me! she said. Then she added: Our candles will go on burning, doing whatever they can, without us.

I stepped off the roundabout, made my way with some difficulty through the traffic and found a café. I went inside, took off my anorak, dried my face on a towel in the toilet and ordered a hot grog. The café was full of people and many of them were particularly well-dressed. I listened, as I sipped the hot liquor, and I heard German and English being spoken. The clientele, I concluded, were probably from the nearby embassies.

So, this morning you went to see Dr Martins. There was a good man! Some of us still go to consult him.

I hear her say this, yet I can't see her. I am sitting alone.

How do they go to consult him, your friends?

His surgery hours are when he's asleep.

Dr Martins died a century ago.

The dead are allowed to sleep too, aren't they?

What do they complain of, your friends who consult him?

Many suffer from hopefulness. Amongst us hopeful-ness is almost as common as depression among the living.

You see hopefulness as an illness?

One of its terminal symptoms is a desire to intervene again in life, and for us that is fatal.

Is there a cure?

Dr Martins prescribes a spell with the martyrs!

It seems he loved women, I tell her.

I'll tell you a story, she says. One day a rich patient asked him to visit her in her large house. He examined her and then asked the maid to fetch him a glass of water from, specifically, the pantry tap. He knew the pantry was far away. During the maid's absence he performed the cure. When the maid returned with the glass of water, he drank it. Doctor, when will your next visit be? asked the woman from her sickbed. He pondered, winked swiftly at his patient, and said: When I'm thirsty, Señora. Upon which Dr Martins left.

She laughs. A crystalline laugh, as if everyone in the café is clinking glasses. Nobody else gives any sign of hearing it.

I see him played by Groucho Marx, she says.

In the Davies Picture Palace the two of us had seen *A Night at the Opera* and *Duck Soup*. Her laughter in the cinema had been muffled as if she didn't want to draw attention to our presence, which bordered on the illicit. Illicit since neither of us mentioned our visits to the Picture Palace to anybody else, and illicit, in a more direct sense, because she contrived and often succeeded in getting us in without paying. A question of narrow uncarpeted stairs and safety exits.

All my books have been about you, I suddenly say.

Nonsense! Maybe you wrote them so I should be there, keeping you company. And I was. Yet they were about everything in the world but me! I've had to wait until now, until you are an old man in Lisboa, for you to be writing this very short story about me.

Books are also about language and language for me is inseparable from your voice.

You're trying to be clever. Don't. Just think of me. Then you'll learn endurance. Something which can only be learnt from a woman, never from a man.

Scott in the Antarctic?

Think of Scott's wife. Her name was Kathleen. 'I regret,' Kathleen said, 'I regret nothing but his suffering.'

Why did you never read any of my books?

I liked books which took me to another life. That's why I read the books I did. Many. Each one was about real life, but not about what was happening to me when I found my bookmark and went on reading. When I read, I lost all sense of time. Women always wonder about other lives, most men are too ambitious to understand this. Other lives, other lives which you have lived before, or which you could have lived. And your books, I hoped, were about another life which I only wanted to imagine, not live, imagine by myself on my own, without any words. So it was better I didn't read them. I could see them through the glass door of the bookcase. That was enough for me.

I risk to write nonsense these days.

You put something down and you don't immediately know what it is. It has always been like that, she says. All you have to know is whether you're lying or whether you're trying to tell the truth, you can't afford to make a mistake about that distinction any longer.

I was thirteen when she had to have all her teeth pulled. She had been brought back home in a taxi. I stood at the door of the bedroom. She lay on her back, chin protruding, cheeks hollow through the new lack of teeth. I knew I had to choose between two things, the only two things I could do at that instant. I could scream or I could go and lie beside her. So I lay beside her. She was too artful to show her pleasure immediately. We both had to wait. After several minutes she pulled an arm out from under the bedclothes and held my wrist in her cold hand. She kept her eyes shut. Most people, she said, can't stand the truth. It's too bad but there it is, most people can't stand it. You, John, I think you can bear the truth, we'll see. Time will tell. I didn't reply. I stayed there on the bed.

Most of the time I'm lost, I tell her in the café with the embassy employees.

That's why you see clearly.

Very little.

Better than me!

She laughs again. A cascading laugh like the sound of a stream that has broken its banks. I hear it as an invitation to dance, to dance on the ruins, so I push back my chair, and with my arms held up like a ballroom dancing partner, I take a step towards where I think she is. The embassy employees look up, mouths open. I sit down. When the general talk resumes, I whisper:

So where do I see you next?

On the aqueduct. The Águas Livres aqueduct.

It's very long, fourteen kilometres, I think.

Where it crosses the Alcântara valley. The arches are sixty metres high at that point. From up there you can almost see America! I'll be waiting for you by the sixteenth arch.

The sixteenth counting which way?

What do you think? From the Mãe d'Agua. I'll meet you there on Tuesday morning.

Not before?

We all have one day in the week that wishes us well.

Which was mine?

It was Tuesday. You will probably die on a Tuesday.

And yours?

Friday. You didn't notice? I must say, I thought you would have noticed.

You weren't there that often.

Far more often than you believed. I wasn't there all the time, which is what you wanted. I wasn't there for ever.

Maybe you did seem happier on Fridays, I say.

43

Not so much a question of being happy, more a question of knowing I was a bit more protected and therefore freer.

When did you discover Friday was your day?

When I was ten; I noticed that if I sang on a Friday I had perfect pitch. Invariably.

Is Friday still your day?

No. Now my day is Tuesday because I'm here for you.

She laughs yet again. An anticipatory laugh. As if she sees the two of us approaching a big joke.

Lisboa is a city of endurance, unanswerable questions and pet names. The Águas Livres aqueduct was completed in 1748. It survived, perfectly intact, the earthquake that destroyed the centre of the city seven years later. When the army engineers planned the aqueduct's course, did they try to avoid the geological fault-lines? Otherwise its exemption remains a mystery. Later, many subsidiary aqueducts were completed and added in order to augment the water supply flowing along the Águas Livres. In reality, the water – as sceptics had warned from the beginning – was never enough for the city.

In the nineteenth century the aqueduct was known as the Passeio dos Arcos, the Road of Arches, because people from the villages in the west walking to the city to sell their produce or their labour, used it as a short cut. They no longer needed to go down into the Alcântara valley, cross the water and climb up; they could just walk one kilometre across the sky. It is said that this is why they gave pet names to the thirty-odd arches of the Alcântara, names like Lia, Adila, Carolina, Sandra, Iracena. And to the great pointed arch in the middle, which is still the highest stone arch in the world, they gave the name of Maira.

The first modern proposal to bring water to the city by an aqueduct – the Romans had tried it before – was prompted, not so much by a concern about hygiene or the population's chronic lack of drinking water, as by the authorities' fear of fire. Every year, in district after district of the city, fires were destroying property.

When the aqueduct was finished the Marquês and bankers arranged to have their own private aqueducts siphoning off the great one. Meanwhile the poor, with no water where they lived, remained at the mercy of the public fountains which, when there was a drought, went dry. Or else they had to buy water from the water-seller at a price they could not afford. This was what the Águas Livres, the so-called Free Water, turned out to be.

Do you always want everything? Her voice interrupts me as I think.

I remember her peeling and slicing cooked beetroots, hands holding the beet, the stubby knife, her stained fingers and the shiny purple crimson of the slices, the intensity of whose colour somehow matched the intensity of her insistence on the immediate and the day-to-day.

As soon as I started enquiring about how I could get up on to the aqueduct, I understood why she had slyly made the rendezvous for the following Tuesday. It was going to take some time. All entrances were locked and one had to apply for official permission from the water company. Even supposing that one had a persuasive reason for asking for permission, there was bound to be some bureaucratic delay. I decided I would claim that I was writing a story about Lisboa.

Do you know the city well? the public relations lady asked me. She was looking worried, as if she had too many exam papers to correct, although clearly she wasn't a teacher. It occurred to me that I should have offered her some *Toicino do Céu*. She would have eaten them absentmindedly while working on her computer.

No, I replied, I love the city but I don't know it well. That's why I need your help.

As you are probably aware, the Águas Livres supplied water to the city until a very few years ago. Now it doesn't but we keep it running as – how do you say? – as a kind of homage? You could go up on Monday morning with Fernando. He's the maintenance inspector for the water channels. 8:30 a.m., here in this office, Monday!

Could it be Tuesday?

Yes, but I thought you said it was urgent.

Tuesday would be better.

Then come Tuesday.

Fernando turned out to be a man in his mid-sixties, on the point of retirement. He had worked all his life for the

46

Empresa Portuguesa das Águas Livres. He kept his eyes screwed up, he held himself very upright for his age, and he had the air of a man used to being alone and away from the crowds – like a shepherd or a steeplejack. He led me very quickly through the imposing temple-like building of the reservoir, which can hold 5,000 cubic metres of water. It was clear he did not like the temple – it had been built for too many people and too many speeches had been made there.

His private passion was for the water on its long, solitary, unnatural, improbable journey from its sources. A journey underground, over ground, and through the sky. Up there in its ducts the water had to be kept cool and well mixed, tranquil, and transparent, with the correct amount of light so that it did not become turgid. As soon as we were on the steps climbing up from the reservoir to the aqueduct, he slowed down.

The aqueduct at its top is only about five metres wide and consists of an apparently endless stone tunnel, on either side of which there is an open, very straight path, with a parapet to prevent people falling off. Fernando considered the water in the aqueduct as something alive, that had to be protected, fed, cleaned out, looked after – almost like an animal in a zoo. Perhaps an otter. Once a week he walked the fourteen kilometres to its sources in the Cavenque, checking everything. I think he had the impression that, like an otter, the water recognised him when he approached. He was dreading his retirement.

By this time we had walked some distance along the

path and were high above the Alcântara valley. With a gesture over the parapet he indicated how he hated the idea of being stuck down there with the crowds, the cows, the chatter. And what made it worse was that he was still fit! He asked me my age. I told him. So you understand! he said. *Você entende*! I understood.

Now he wanted to show me his tunnel. He explained how the two semi-circular ducts for channelling the water were carved by hand out of basalt stone, piece by piece, and how the blocks were fitted together with mortice and tenon joints, and the cracks between the blocks filled with a putty made of quicklime, powdered limestone, and virgin olive oil, and how this putty, once set, was tougher than the basalt stone. Fernando had been trained as a stonemason.

I could not accompany him because of my rendezvous. Nor did I want him to be there when I met my mother. The other times the presence of others hadn't worried me. Perhaps it was something to do with the location, with being off the ground. Or perhaps because it was the only time my mother had fixed the meeting in advance.

I told him I wanted to draw the view and to draw I needed to be quiet. He nodded, and unlocked a door that led into the tunnel, saying he would leave it open, so that when I was finished I could come and find him.

As he stepped out of the sunlight into the vaulted obscurity, his face relaxed and his eyes opened. The tunnel inside was narrow. I could easily have touched both walls with my outstretched arms. The semi-circular channels on either side were about two hand-spans in diameter.

They were less than half-full, yet the flow of the water was even and persistent. After many kilometres, the water had become convinced of the gradient.

Down the centre, above the ducts, ran a flagged walkway, straight as a die, as far as the eye could see. It too was narrow. Two people would have had considerable difficulty in passing on it without one of them stepping off. Fernando switched on his lamp and set out.

A little later, while I was leaning against the parapet opposite the door he had left open, I thought I heard him talking. He was speaking in brief sentences as if making or giving notes. Yet there was nobody with him.

I started walking fast down the outside path, enticed on by the aqueduct's straightness. All Vieira da Silva's paintings are, in some way, about Lisboa and its skies and the paths through its skies. When I reached the far side of the valley I turned back and counted the arches until I found the sixteenth, which was not far from Fernando's open door.

Way below were a couple of unfinished streets and some houses which were being lived in, though still being built. A poor suburb rather than a *favela*. I could see a car with no wheels, a balcony the size of a kitchen chair, a child's swing with only one rope attached to a tree, red tiles with concrete blocks on them to prevent them being blown away by the Atlantic winds, a window without a frame with a double mattress hanging out of it, a dog on a chain, barking in the sun.

Do you see? she suddenly said. Everything is broken,

slightly broken, like the rejects from the factory they sell cheap, at half price. Not really damaged, only rejects. Everything – the hills, the Sea of Straw, the child's swing down there, the car, the castle, everything is a reject, and has been so since the beginning.

She was sitting on a portable stool a few metres along the path from me. It was a stool with three legs that folded, which was very light; she used to carry it with her so she could sit down in public places. She was wearing a cloche hat.

Everything begins sour, she said, then goes sweet and is afterwards bitter.

Did Father enjoy his swordfish? I asked.

I'm talking about life, not about details.

In spite of her words she was smiling, even her shoulders were smiling. I remember her smiling like that in a bathing costume on a beach around 1935, because whilst she was wearing the bathing costume she considered herself spared from work.

There was a mistake at the beginning, she continued. Everything began with a death.

I don't understand.

One day, when you're in my situation, you will. The Creation began with a death.

Two white butterflies were circling above her hat. Perhaps they had come with her, for there is little on the aqueduct at that height to attract butterflies.

Surely, I asked, the beginning might be thought of as a birth?

That's the common error, and you fell into the trap as I thought you would!

So, everything began with a death, you say!

Exactly. And the births followed. The births happened – that's why there's birth – precisely because they offered a chance of repairing some of what was damaged from the beginning, after the death. That's why we are here, John. To repair.

Yet you are not really here, are you?

How stupid can you get! We – us – we are all here. Just like you and the living are here. You and us, we are here to repair a little of what was broken. This is why we occurred.

Occurred?

Came to be.

You talk as if nobody can choose anything!

Choose whatever you like. What you can't do is to hope for everything.

She was still beaming.

Of course.

Hope is a great magnifier – which is why it doesn't see far ahead.

Why are you smiling?

Let's hope only for what has some chance of being achieved! Let a few things be repaired. A few is a lot. One thing repaired changes a thousand others.

So?

The dog down there is on too short a chain. Change it, lengthen it. Then he'll be able to reach the shade, and he'll lie down and he'll stop barking. And the silence will remind the mother she wanted a canary in a cage in the kitchen. And when the canary sings, she'll do more ironing. And the father's shoulders in a freshly ironed shirt will ache less when he goes to work. And so when he comes home he'll sometimes joke, like he used to, with his teenage daughter. And the daughter will change her mind and decide, just this once, to bring her lover home one evening. And on another evening, the father will propose to the young man that they go fishing together . . . Who in the wide world knows? Just lengthen the chain.

The dog was still barking.

There are certain things which, to be repaired, require nothing short of a revolution, I suggest.

So you say, John.

It's not a question of my saying, it's a question of circumstances.

I prefer to believe it's your saying.

Why?

It's less evasive. Circumstances! Anything can hide behind that word. I believe in repairs, as I was telling you, and one other thing.

What would that be?

The inevitability of desire. Desire cannot be stopped.

At this point she got up from her portable stool and leant against the parapet.

Desire is unstoppable. The other day I heard one of us explaining why. But I knew it before. Think of a bottomless pit, think of a nothing. An absolute nothing. In it there's already an appeal – are you following me? A Nothing is an appeal for Something. It can't be otherwise. Yet the appeal is all there is; there's only a naked crying-out appeal. A yearning. And so we come to the eternal conundrum of making something out of nothing.

She took a step towards me. She was whispering, with her bathing-costume smile, and her brown eyes fixed on some point in the distance.

The something which is made can give no support to anything else, it is only a desire. It possesses nothing, nothing is given to it, there is no place for it! Yet it exists! It exists. He was a shoemaker, I believe, the man who said all this.

Sounds to me like Jacob Boehme.

Stop dropping names!

She laughed her impertinent seventeen-year-old laugh.

Stop dropping names! she repeated and giggled. From here you could kill somebody dropping a name!

We gazed down at the red tiles and the double mattress in the window. The dog had stopped barking. And, when she stopped laughing, I held her cold hand.

Just write down what you find, she said.

I'll never know what I've found.

No, you'll never know.

It takes courage to write, I said.

The courage will come. Write down what you find, and do us the courtesy of noticing us.

You are no longer here!

Hence, the courtesy, John!

After saying this, she got to her feet, handed me the folding stool and proceeded to the door that Fernando had left unlocked. There she tugged it open and stepped – as if she had done the same thing every morning of her life – over the water duct, up on to the narrow flagged walkway.

Inside the air was cooler – as if we were underground instead of being in the sky. The light too was different. Outside, the daylight had been sparkling and transparent; having penetrated the tunnel, it changed and became golden. Every fifty metres the vaulted roof opened out into a small tower, which was built like a stone lantern so that daylight could enter. And from each lantern, as one after another they receded into the distance, the daylight fell like a golden curtain, the curtains getting forever smaller. Sound was also different. In the quiet we heard the lapping – as discrete as a cat's tongue when drinking – of water flowing down the two basalt-stone channels on its way to the Mãe d'Agua.

I'm not sure how long we stood there facing each other – perhaps for the fifteen years since her death.

After the death of mothers, time often doubles or accelerates its speed.

Eventually she turned round, bit her lower lip, and began to walk. As she did so, she repeated without looking back: The courtesy, John!

She approached the cascade of light from the first stone lantern. Either side of her, the water reflected sparks that bobbed up and down like floating candles. When she entered the gold, it hid her like a curtain, and I did not see her again until she re-emerged from the light on the far side. She had become small because of the distance. She seemed to be walking with increasing ease; the further away she got, the more sprightly she became. She disappeared into the next golden curtain and when she re-appeared I could scarcely distinguish her.

I bent down and I let my hand trail in the water which was flowing after her.

2

Genève

There's a photo of Jorge Luis Borges, probably taken in the early 1980s, a year or two before he left Buenos Aires to come to die in Genève, a city he claimed as one of his 'native lands'. You can see in the photo how he's almost blind and you sense how blindness is a prison – something he often referred to in his poetry. At the same time, his face in this photo is one inhabited by many other lives. It is a face full of company; many other men and women with their appetites speak through his almost sightless eyes. A face of countless desires. It's a portrait which might be lent to the poets across the centuries and millennia, indexed as 'Anonymous'.

The city of Genève is as contradictory and enigmatic as a living person. I could fill in an identity card. *Nationality:* Neutral. *Gender:* Feminine. *Age:* (discretion intervenes) Looks younger than she is. *Civil status:* Separated. *Occupation:* Observer. *Distinguishing physical characteristic:* Slight stoop due to short-sightedness. *General remarks:* Sexy and secretive.

The only other European town whose natural situation may be as breathtaking is Toledo. (The towns themselves are utterly different.) In thinking of Toledo, however, I'm influenced by El Greco's painting of the town; whereas Genève has never been painted to any effect by anybody, and her only symbol is a toy water-spout shooting up out of the lake, which she turns off and on like a halogen lamp.

In the sky over Genève, the clouds – depending upon the winds, of which the two most notorious are the *bise* and the *foehn* – come from Italy, Austria, France, or, down the Rhine valley from Germany, the Low Countries, and the Baltic. Sometimes they come from as far away as North Africa and Poland. Genève is a place of convergence, and she knows it.

For centuries travellers passing through have left letters, instructions, maps, lists, messages, for Genève to deliver to other travellers arriving later. She reads them all with a mixture of curiosity and pride. Those unfortunate enough not to be born in our canton, she concludes, are apparently obliged to live out every one of their passions, and passion is a blinding misfortune. Her central Post Office was designed to be as imposing as her Cathedral.

At the beginning of the twentieth century Genève was a regular meeting point for European revolutionaries and conspirators – just as today it is one of the rendezvous of the new world economic order. More permanently, it hosts the International Red Cross, the

United Nations, the International Labour Office, the World Health Organization, the Ecumenical Council of Churches. Forty per cent of the population is foreign. Twenty-five thousand people live and work there without papers. At the UN about twenty-four men are employed full-time simply to carry files and letters from one department to another.

To the revolutionary conspirators, to the troubled international negotiators, and to the financial mafiosi of today, Genève has offered, and continues to offer, tranquility, her white wine tasting of fossilised sea shells, her trips on the lake, snow, beautiful pears, sunsets reflected in the water, hoar frost on the trees at least once a year, the safest lifts in the world, Arctic fish from her lake, milk chocolate, and a comfort which is so unceasing, discreet and accomplished that it becomes lecherous.

In the summer of 1914, when Borges was fifteen, his family, on a visit from the Argentine, found themselves trapped in Genève by the outbreak of war. Borges went to school at the Collège Calvin. His sister attended the art school. It was probably while he was walking between the Rue Ferdinand-Hodler, where they had an apartment, and the Collège Calvin, that he composed his first poems.

The Genevois themselves frequently get bored with their town, fondly bored – they seldom dream of freeing themselves and leaving her for good, rather they find their excitement in travelling far and wide.

They are enterprising, often intrepid, travellers. A city full of travellers' tales, told around dinner tables she has laid and decorated with her usual meticulous care, with never, as it were, a single spelling mistake, each dish always ready on time and served with a non-committal smile.

Despite her direct descent from Calvin, nothing she hears or witnesses shocks her. Nothing tempts her either, or rather nothing which is obvious. Her secret passion (for of course she has one) is well hidden and discerned by only a few.

On the southern side of Genève, very close to the Rhône as it flows out of the lake, there are a number of narrowish, shortish, straight streets of four-storey buildings, built in the nineteenth century originally as residential apartments. Some were later turned into offices, others are still used as flats.

These streets lead like the aisles which run between the bookshelves of an extensive library. As seen from the street, each line of shut windows is the glass door to another bookshelf. The closed front doors of varnished wood are the drawers of the library catalogue. Behind these walls everything is waiting to be read. I call them her archive streets.

They have nothing to do with the town's official archives of committee reports, forgotten memos, resolutions passed, minutes of a million meetings, findings of obscure researchers, desperate public appeals, the first drafts of speeches with love doodles in the margin, prophecies so accurate they had to be buried, complaints about interpreters, and endless annual budgets – all these are stored elsewhere in the offices of the International Organisations. What is waiting to be read on the shelves in the archive streets is private, unprecedented and almost weightless.

Archives are different from book libraries. Libraries are made up of bound volumes, whose every page has been repeatedly reread and corrected. Archives often consist of papers which were originally abandoned or laid aside. Genève's passion is for discovering, cataloguing and checking what has been laid aside. No wonder she's short-sighted. No wonder she arms herself – even when asleep – against pity.

For example, how to catalogue a small page torn from a desk calendar, covering the two weeks from Sunday 22 September to Saturday 5 October in the year 1935? In the small space for notes, between the columns of the two weeks, are written eleven words. The handwriting is sloping and quick and unconsidered. Perhaps a woman's. The words, in English, are: *all night, all night and what is it on a postcard*.

What does Genève's passion bring her? It assuages her insatiable curiosity. A curiosity which has nothing – or very little – to do with inquisitiveness or gossip. She is neither concierge, nor judge. Genève is an observer, fascinated by the sheer variety of human predicaments and consolations.

Confronted with any situation, however outrageous,

she is capable of muttering 'I know' and then of adding gently: Sit there, I'll see what I can bring you.

Impossible to guess whether what she will bring will come from a bookshelf, a medicine chest, a cellar, a wardrobe or the drawer of her bedside table. And strangely, it is this question about the provenance of what she will bring that makes her sexy.

When he was seventeen, Borges had an experience in Genève which marked him deeply. He only spoke about it much later to one or two friends. His father had decided it was high time his son lost his virginity. Accordingly he arranged an appointment for him with a prostitute. A bedroom on a second floor. A late spring afternoon. Near to where the family lived. Perhaps in the Place du Bourg-de-Four, perhaps in the Rue du Général-Dufour. Borges may have confused the two names. I would opt for the Rue du Général-Dufour because it is an archive street.

Face to face with the prostitute, the seventeen-year-old Borges was paralysed by shyness, shame and the suspicion that his father was a client of the same woman. Throughout his life his own body distressed him. He undressed only in poems, which, at the same time, were his clothes.

When the woman noticed the young man's distress, that afternoon in the Rue du Général-Dufour, she threw a peignoir over her white shoulders and, stooping slightly, walked over towards the door.

Sit there, she said gently. I'll see what I can bring you.

What she brought was something she found in one of the archives.

Many years later, when Borges was the Director of the National Library in Buenos Aires, his imagination became the tireless collector of put-aside objects, torn telltale notes, mislaid fragments. His great poetic oeuvre is a kind of catalogue of the items of such a collection: some man's memory of a woman who left him thirty years ago, a ring of keys, a deck of cards, a withered violet crushed between the pages of a book, the mirrored letter on a blotting paper, a fallen volume hidden from sight by the other volumes, a symmetric rose in a boy's kaleidoscope, the colours of a Turner when the lights are turned out in the narrow gallery, fingernails, atlases, a moustache greying at the ends, the oars of Argus . . .

Sit there, I'll see what I can bring you.

Last summer while Bush and his army and the petrol corporations and their advisors were ruining Iraq, I had a rendezvous in Genève with my daughter, Katya. I had told Katya about the encounter with my mother in Lisboa. When my mother was alive she and Katya had an understanding, for they shared something quite deep, which they didn't have to discuss. Both agreed that to find any sense in life it was pointless to search in the places where people were instructed to look. Sense was only to be found in secrets.

After listening to the story of what happened in Lisboa, Katya proposed: Your courtesy can begin with Borges! Why not? You quote him, we discuss him, we've often talked about visiting the cemetery, and you never have, let's go together!

She was working in the Grand Théâtre de Genève, so I drove there to pick her up. As soon as I switched off the engine and put my feet down, the heat was stifling. I pulled off my gloves. There was almost no traffic. Everyone in the city centre leaves in high summer. The few pedestrians, mostly elderly, had the assured slow rhythm of sleepwalkers. They preferred to be outside rather than in their apartments, for such heat is even more oppressive when you face it alone. They meandered, they sat, they fanned themselves, and they licked ice creams or ate apricots. (It was the best summer for apricots for a decade.)

I took off my helmet and stuffed my gloves into it.

Motorbikers wear light leather gloves even on the hottest summer days for a special reason. Nominally gloves are for protection in case of a fall, and to isolate the hands from the sticky rubber of the grips. More intimately, however, they shield the hands from the cool air-rush which, although highly agreeable in the heat, blunts the sensitivity of touch. Riders wear summer gloves on their hands for the pleasure of precision.

I went to the stage door and asked for Katya. The receptionist was drinking iced tea (peach flavour) from a tin. The theatre was shut for a month, and there was only a basic working staff.

Sit there, the receptionist said gently, and I'll see if I can find her.

Katya's job was to write programme notes explaining opera and ballet to school classes – including the pupils of the Collège Calvin. When she came running down the stairs from her office, she was wearing a printed summer dress of charcoal-black and white. Borges would have seen only a smudged grey blur.

I didn't keep you waiting?

Never.

Do you want to see the stage? We can climb right up to the top, it's very high, and then look down on the whole empty theatre.

There's something about empty theatres . . .

Yes, they are full!

We started up a metal staircase like an outdoor fire escape. Above us two or three stagehands were controlling the mechanism of the lights. She waved at them.

They invited me, she said, and I told them I'd bring you too.

They waved back at her, laughing.

Later, when we arrived at their level, one of them said to Katya: So, see you've got a good head for heights!

And I wondered how many times in my life I had taken part in the ritual of men showing to women the special little risks they run while working. (When the risks are large they don't show them.) They want

65

to impress, they want to be admired. It's a pretext for holding the women to show them where to step or how to bend. There's another pleasure too. The ritual exaggerates the difference between women and men and in that expanded difference there is a fluttering of hopes. For an hour or two afterwards the routine feels lighter.

How high are we?

Nearly a hundred metres, sweetie-pie.

Faintly, from some rehearsal room, we heard the trilling of a soprano warming her voice. Away from the dimmed battery of lights, everything was dark except for an open door, no larger than a hatchway, far below, at the back of the stage. Sunlight streamed through it. It had undoubtedly been opened to let in a little air. The stagehands were in shorts and vests and we were sweating.

The soprano began an aria.

Bellini's *I Puritani*, the youngest stagehand announced. Eighty performances last season!

> *O rendetemi la speme*
> *O lasciatemi morir . . .*

> Let me hope again
> Or let me die.

The stage was as large as a dry dock and Katya and I walked off along one of the bridges. Hanging parallel to

66

the bridge, and descending right down to the boards of the stage, were the painted decors of the season's repertoire.

A beam from a spotlight tracked across the boards; the voice, for some reason, stopped in mid-song, and it was at that moment that we saw a bird fly in through the open door, way below.

For several minutes it circled the dark space. Then it perched, confused, on a cable. We saw it was a starling. It headed towards the lights, believing they were exits into the sunshine. It had forgotten or could not refind the doorway it had come in by.

It flew between the hanging backdrops of Sea, Mountain, Spanish Inn, German Forest, Royal Palace, Peasant Wedding. And as it flew it cried Tcheeer! Tcheeer! more and more shrilly as it realised more and more surely that it was trapped.

Trapped birds need everything to go dark except their path of escape. This didn't happen and so the starling hurtled against walls, curtains and canvas. Tcheeer! Tcheeer! Tcheeer!

There is an old opera-house superstition that if a bird is killed on stage, the building will catch fire.

The rehearsing soprano, in trousers and a T-shirt, came on stage. Perhaps someone had told her about the bird.

Tcheeer! Tcheeer! imitated Katya. The singer looked up and cottoned on. She too imitated the starling's cry. The bird responded. The singer improved her pitch and the two cries became almost indistinguishable. The bird flew towards her.

Katya and I hurried down the metal stairs. As we passed the stagehands the young one said to Katya: Didn't know you were a diva!

Outside in the street, at the corner of the theatre where the little door opened, the soprano, hands clasped before her, repeatedly sang: Tcheeer! Tcheeer! The elderly people with their ice creams and apricots were gathered around her, unsurprised. In such heat, in a deserted city, anything can happen.

Let's have an espresso first, Katya said, then go to the cemetery.

She found a place fully in the sun. I sat in the shade. We heard clapping in the distance. Perhaps the bird had flown out. Who would believe us, she said, if we told the story?

The cemetery had wide lawns and tall trees. A thrush was stepping fastidiously over some newly mown grass. We asked a gardener, who was Bosnian, for directions.

We found the grave at last in a far corner. A simple headstone, and a rectangle of gravel on which was placed a wickerwork basket containing earth and a thick, small-leafed, very dark green shrub with berries. I must find out its name, for Borges loved exactitude; it gave him the possibility, when writing, of landing precisely where he chose. All his life he was scandalously or grievously lost in politics, but never on the page he was writing on.

Debo justificar lo que me hiere.
No importa mi ventura o mi desventura.
Soy el poeta.

I have to justify what wounds me.
My fortune or misfortune does not matter.
I am the poet.

The shrub, according to the Bosnian gardener, was *Buxus sempervivens*. I should have recognised it. In the villages of the Haute-Savoie one dips a sprig of this plant into holy water to sprinkle blessings for the last time on the corpse of the loved one laid out on the bed. It became a holy plant because of a shortage. On Palm Sunday there were never enough willow leaves available in the region, and so the Savoyards started to use the evergreen box instead.

He died, the gravestone announced, on June 14th 1986.

The two of us stood there in silence. Katya had a handbag hanging over her shoulder and I was holding my black crash helmet into which I had stuffed my gloves. We bent down to crouch over the gravestone.

On it was a low-relief carving of men in what looked like a medieval boat. Or were they on land and was it their warrior discipline that made them stand so close and steadfastly together? They looked ancient. On the back of the gravestone were other warriors, holding either lances or oars, confident, ready to cross whatever terrain or water had to be crossed.

When Borges came to Genève to die, he was accompanied by María Kodama. In the early sixties she had been one of his students studying Anglo-Saxon and Norse literature. She was half his age. When they got married, eight weeks before he died, they moved out of a hotel in an archive street called the Rue de la Tour-Maîtresse, into an apartment she had found.

This book, he wrote in a dedication, is yours, María Kodama. Must I say to you that this inscription includes twilights, the deer of Nara, night that is alone and populated mornings, shared islands, seas, deserts, and gardens, what forgetting loses and memory transforms, the high-pitched voice of the muezzin, the death of Hawkwood, some books and engravings? . . . We can only give what we have given. We can only give what is already the other's!

A young man with his son in a pushchair walked past while Katya and I were trying to decide what language the engraved inscription was in. The little boy pointed at a pigeon who strutted forward, and bubbled over with laughter, sure that it was he who had made the bird move.

The four words on the front of the stela were, we discovered, in Anglo-Saxon. *And Ne Forhtedan Na.* Should Not Be Afraid.

A couple approached an empty bench further down the

cemetery path. They hesitated and then decided to sit. The woman sat on her man's knees, facing him.

The words on the back were in Norse. *Hann tekr sverthit Gram ok leggr i methal theira bert.* He takes the sword Gram and lays it naked between them. The sentence comes from a Norse saga that Kodama and Borges loved over the years and played games with.

At the very bottom of the stela, near the grass, is written: From Ulrike to Javier Otárola. Ulrike was the name Borges lent Kodama, and Javier the name she lent him.

It's a shame, I thought to myself, that we didn't bring any flowers to leave. Then I had an idea: instead of flowers, I would leave one of my leather gloves.

The gardener driving his lawnmower was getting closer. I could hear the two-stroke engine and smell the newly cut grass. I know of no other smell which has as much to do with beginnings: morning, childhood, spring.

> The memory of a morning.
> Lines of Virgil and Frost.
> The voice of Macedonio Fernándéz.
> The love or the conversation of a few people.
> Certainly they are talismans, but useless against
>   the dark I cannot name,
>   the dark I must not name.

I began to wonder. The glove will only look as if somebody has dropped it! A crumpled black dropped

glove! It will mean nothing. Forget it. Better come back
another day with a bouquet of flowers. What flowers?

O endless rose, intimate, without limit,
Which the Lord will finally show to my dead eyes.

Katya looked at me enquiringly. I nodded. It was time
to go. We walked slowly back towards the gate, neither of
us speaking.

You found the one you were looking for? asked the
Bosnian gardener.

Thanks to you, replied Katya.

Family?

Yes family, she said.

Outside the theatre everything was calm and the door
of the starling's flight was closed. I had parked my bike
next to Katya's scooter. She went to fetch her helmet.
About to put on my own, I pulled out the gloves. There
was only one. I looked again. Only one.

What's the matter?

There's a glove missing.

You must have dropped it, we'll go back, it'll only take
a minute.

I told her what had gone through my head as we were
standing by the grave.

You underestimated him, she said conspiratorially,
gravely underestimated him.

While we were laughing, I stuffed the remaining glove
into my pocket and she climbed up behind me. Most of

the lights were green and we were soon over the Rhône, leaving the city behind and taking the chicane bends up to the pass. The warm air rushed over my bare hands and Katya leant into the turns. I remembered how she had recently quoted Zeno of Elea in an SMS message to me: What is in motion is neither in the space where it is, nor in the space where it isn't; for me this is a definition of music.

We made a sort of music until we reached the Col de la Faucille.

There we stopped and got off to look down at the lake, towards the Alps, and at the city of Genève with its multitude of lifetimes.

3

Kraków

It was not a hotel. It was a kind of *pension* where, at the most, there were four or five guests. In the morning breakfast on a tray was placed on a shelf in the corridor: bread, butter, honey and slices of a sausage which is a speciality of the city. Beside the tray, packets of Nescafé and an electric water heater. Contact with the severe and serene young women who ran the place was minimal.

In the bedrooms all the furniture, made of either oak or walnut, was old and must have dated from before the Second World War. This was in the only Polish city which survived that war without serious destruction to its buildings. In the *pension*, as in a convent or a monastery, there was a sense inside each room that the two windows which gave on to the streets had been contemplatively looked through for several generations.

The building was situated on Miodowa Street in Kazimierz, the old Jewish quarter of Kraków. After breakfast I asked a young woman behind the reception desk where the nearest bankomat was. She regretfully put down the violin case she was holding and picked up a tourist map of the city. On it she marked in pencil where I had to go. It's not far, she sighed, as if she would have liked to send me to the other side of the world. I bowed discreetly, opened and shut the front door, turned right, took the first right again and found myself in the Place Nowy, an open market-square.

I have never been in this square before and I know it by heart, or rather I know by heart the people who are selling things in it. Some of them have regular stalls with awnings to keep the sun off their goods. It is already hot, hot with the blurred, gnat heat of the Eastern European plains and forest. A foliage heat. A heat full of suggestions, that does not have the assurance of a Mediterranean heat. Here nothing is certain. The nearest thing to certainty here is a grandmother.

Other sellers – all of them women – have come from the outlying villages with their own produce in baskets or buckets. They do not have stalls and are sitting on stools they brought with them. A few stand. I wander between them.

Lettuces, red radishes, horseradishes, cut dill like green lace, small knobby cucumbers which in this heat grow in three days, new potatoes, their skins, with a little powdered earth on them, the colour of grandchildren's knees, stick-celery with its cleansing toothbrush smell, cuttings of liveche, which the men, drinking vodka, swear is an incomparable aphrodisiac for women as well as men, bunches of young carrots swapping fern jokes, cut roses mostly yellow, cottage cheeses, which the rags pegged to the clothes line in their gardens still smell of, wild green asparagus that the children were sent to look for near the village cemetery.

The professional traders have naturally acquired all the trading tricks for persuading the public that golden opportunities never come twice. The women on their stools, by contrast, propose nothing. They are immobile, expressionless, and rely on their own simple presence to guarantee the quality of what they have brought to sell from their own gardens.

A wooden fence around a plot and a two-roomed house made from logs with a single tiled stove between the two rooms. These women live in *chatas* like this.

I wander between them. Different ages. Different builds. Eyes of different colour. No two women wearing the same kerchief. And each one of them has found, as she bends down to cut chives or pull out dog-tooth weed or pick red radishes, her own way of protecting, of favouring, the small of her back, so that its intermittent aches do not become chronic. When they were younger it was their hips which absorbed the shock of events, now it is their shoulders which have to do so.

I peer into the basket of a woman who is standing without a stool. The basket is full of pale golden pastries, little pies. They look like carved chessmen, more specifically, like castles, castles that could be stood either way up, their regular embrasures always at the top. Each one is ten centimetres tall.

I pick up one of the castles and realise my mistake. It is far too heavy to be made of pastry.

I glance up at the face of the woman. Sixty years old, blue-green eyes. She looks back at me severely, as if at an idiot who has once again forgotten something. *Oscypek*, she says slowly, repeating the proper name of a cheese made from the milk of mountain sheep and smoked in the chimney between the two rooms. I buy three. Then, with the smallest gesture of her head, she suggests I get on my way.

In the centre of the square stands a low building, subdivided into small, round shops. There is a barber's with just enough space for one chair. Several butchers'. A grocer's where you can buy pickled cabbage from a single barrel. A kitchen for soup with a cast-iron stove, and, outside on the paving stones, three wooden tables with benches. At one of the tables sits a man with slightly dejected shoulders, long hands and a high forehead made higher by the fact that he is going bald. His spectacles have thick lenses. He looks at home here this morning, although he is not Polish.

Ken was born in New Zealand and died there. I sit on the bench opposite him. This man, sixty years ago, shared with me what he knew, although he never told me how he learnt what he knew. He never spoke about his childhood or his parents. I had the impression he left

New Zealand for Europe when he was young, before he was twenty. Were his parents rich or poor? Maybe it makes as little sense to ask that question of him as it would of the people in this market at this moment.

Distances never daunted him. Wellington, New Zealand, Paris, New York, the Bayswater Road, London, Norway, Spain, and at some moment, I think, Burma or India. He earned his living, variously, as a journalist, a schoolteacher, a dance instructor, an extra in films, a gigolo, a bookseller without a shop, a cricket umpire. Maybe some of what I'm saying is false, yet it is my way of making a portrait of him for myself as he sits in front of me in the Place Nowy. In Paris he drew cartoons for a newspaper, of this I am certain. I remember distinctly the kind of toothbrushes he liked – ones with extra long handles, and I remember the size of shoe he took – an eleven.

He pushes his bowl of borsch towards me. Then he takes a handkerchief from his right trouser pocket, wipes the spoon and hands it to me. I recognise the handkerchief of black tartan. The soup is a clear, deep, red, vegetable borsch, with a little apple vinegar added to it, Polish-style, to counteract the natural sweetness of the beetroot. I drink some and push the bowl back to him and hand him back the spoon. Not a word has passed between us.

From the bag slung over my shoulder I take out a sketchbook, for I want to show him a drawing I made yesterday from Leonardo's *Lady with an Ermine* in the

Czartoryski Museum. He studies it, his heavy glasses slipping a little down his nose.

Pas mal! Yet isn't she too upright? Isn't she in fact leaning more as she takes the corner?

On hearing him speak in this way, which is so indisputably his, my love for him comes back: my love for his journeys; for his appetites, which he set out to satisfy and never suppressed; for his weariness; for his sad curiosity.

A little too upright, he repeats. Never mind, every copy has to change something, doesn't it?

My love for his lack of illusions comes back too. Without illusions, he avoided disillusionment.

When I first met him I was eleven and he forty. For the next six or seven years he was the most influential person in my life. It was with him that I learnt to cross frontiers. In French there is the word *passeur* – often translated as ferryman or smuggler. Yet there is also in the word the connotation of guide, and something of the mountains. He was my *passeur*.

Ken flips backwards through the sketchbook. He had deft fingers and could palm cards skilfully. He tried to teach me Find the Lady: You can always make money with that! he said. Now he puts a finger between two pages and stops.

Another copy? Antonello da Messina?

Dead Christ supported by Angel, I say.

I never saw it, only in reproduction. If I could have chosen to have my portrait painted by any artist in history, I'd have chosen him, he says. Antonello. He painted like he was printing words. Everything he painted had that kind of coherence and authority, and it was during his lifetime that the first printing presses were invented.

He looks down again at the sketchbook.

Not a trace of pity on the angel's face or in his hands, he says, only tenderness. You've caught that tenderness, but not the gravity, the gravity of the first printed words. That's gone for good.

I did it last year in the Prado. Until the guards came to chuck me out!

Anyone has the right to draw there, no?

Yes, but not to sit on the floor.

Then why didn't you draw standing up!

When Ken says this in the Place Nowy, I see him, tall, stooped, standing on the edge of a cliff making a sketch of the sea. Near Brighton, the summer of 1939. He always carried in his pocket a large black graphite pencil called a Black Prince, which, instead of being round, was rectangular like a carpenter's pencil.

I'm too old now, I tell him, to draw for a long time standing up.

He puts down the sketchbook abruptly without glancing at me. He abhorred self-pity. The weakness, he said, of many intellectuals. Avoid it! This was the only moral imperative he ever imparted to me.

He fingers one of the cheeses I have bought.

Her name is Jagusia, he says, nodding towards the woman who sold me the *oscypek*, and she comes from the mountains in Podhale. Her two sons work in Germany.

Black labour. Hard for them to get work permits, they're forced to be illegal. *Néanmoins*, they're building a house, a house larger than Jagusia has even dreamt of, not one storey but three, not two rooms but seven!

Néanmoins! French words cropped up in his sentences not out of affectation but because the years he had lived in Paris before coming to London and the Bayswater Road, were the happiest of his life. It was for the same reason that he sometimes wore a black beret.

Yet Jagusia will refuse, he prophesies, to move out of her *chata*, with the cheesecloths on the line in the garden.

This was the man who made me believe that together we could find music in any city in the world.

What about a beer? he says now in Kraków, pointing towards the far end of the market building, beyond a clothes shop belonging to a fat woman who is sitting smoking in an armchair, surrounded by dresses.

I get up and walk towards her. As she smokes, she tells the story of what happened when she arrived in the Place Nowy; every morning she does this, and every morning the man who sells dried and pickled mushrooms listens to her, his face expressionless. When all the dresses and trousers she has on display are folded up and stacked in the little shop, there is no space for her. On the inside of the door there is a long mirror, since customers sometimes use it as a changing room. Each morning when she opens the shop, she sees herself in this mirror and each morning she is surprised by her size.

I spot the cans of beer on a stall with dried beans, Polish mustard, biscuits, honey-bread and tinned meats. There is also an open chessboard and a game in progress. The grocer behind the stand is playing Black, and a man who looks like a passer-by is playing White. Several pawns, a knight and a bishop have been taken.

The grocer studies the chessboard from a distance, then turns away and gets on with his job until the other one has made his move. The other one hovers above the game and rocks forwards and backwards on his feet, as if he were one of his own bishops, already lifted very slightly off the board between the fingers of a giant player who is cautiously trying out possible moves, being careful not to relinquish the piece until he is certain.

I ask for two beers. White moves his queen diagonally and says Check! Black takes my money and moves a knight. The queen withdraws. A woman customer asks for some of the honey-bread which has sweet candied oranges buried in it. Black cuts the slices and weighs them. White makes a careless move and realises it too late. He swallows hard, for he has an acid taste in his throat. Black takes a castle.

Kraków's Jewish ghetto, on the other side of the Vistula, outside the old city, is from here less than ten minutes walk over the Most Powstancôw bridge. The ghetto covered an area of 600m × 400m and was sealed off by walled-up buildings, blockades and barbed wire. In the autumn of 1941, six months after it was sealed off,

18,000 people were imprisoned there. Thousands died from disease and malnutrition each month. Only those fit enough to work as slave labour in the German armament or clothes workshops were permitted to leave for their stints of work. All other Jews found trespassing outside the ghetto were shot, as were any Poles who helped them to pass into Aryan Kraków or who hid them.

Tyskie! Ken applauds when I return to the table. You chose the best beer!

Early training! I say.

He's called Zedrek, Ken says, the man you were watching playing chess. He comes to play with Abram the grocer at least once a week. Zedrek could play a good game if he didn't start drinking vodka so early. I don't think he can stop though. Abram as a small boy survived the war in hiding.

Ken taught me most of the games I know: chess, snooker, darts, billiards, poker, table tennis, backgammon. Chess we played in his bed-sitting rooms, the others in bars. Bridge, which I had learnt before I met him, we played with my parents or when we got invited to somebody's house, which was not often.

I met him in 1937. He was a replacement teacher in the lunatic boarding school to which I had been bundled. In front of the school assembly – fifty bare-kneed cowed boys, each trying to find, unaided, a sense to life – the apoplectic headmaster threw a dining-room chair at the Latin teacher and Ken, who happened to be between them, caught it with one hand in mid-flight. This is how I first noticed him. He set the chair down on the podium, put his feet up on it, and the boss continued to harangue.

In the final day of that same term I invited him to a caravan my parents had on a beach near Selsea Bill in Sussex. Why not? he said. And he came for a week.

My father was pleased, for, now making a foursome, we could play bridge together.

Shall we play for money, Sir? asked Ken. Otherwise the bids don't count.

Agreed, but the stakes shouldn't be too high, because of John here.

Tuppence a hundred?

I'll go and fetch my purse, said my mother.

Ken shuffled the pack and the cards cascaded between his two hands held far apart. Sometimes the cascade looked like a moving staircase, an escalator or a playing-cards ladder. Once, later, he said to me, when I was complaining of not being able to go to sleep: Imagine you're shuffling a pack of cards! That's how I go to sleep.

Cut for deal.

My father enjoyed the game, not only because he was a good player, but, more, because the game allowed him to recall certain easy moments with the dead, who otherwise haunted him. When the four of us were playing in Selsea, 'Six Diamonds Doubled' took precedence over 'Five Mortars Lost'. He was playing with us, but also with a roll of infantry officers of which he was the only survivor after four years in the trenches near Vimy Ridge and Ypres.

My mother quickly recognised that Ken belonged to what for her was the special category of 'people who loved Paris'.

Watching the three of us playing quoits on the sand, she foresaw, I'm sure, that the *passeur* was going to take me a long way away and, at the same time, she didn't doubt, I'm equally sure, that, give or take a little, I was capable of looking after myself. Consequently, she offered on Monday, Wash Day, to launder and iron his clothes, and Ken bought her a bottle of Dubonnet.

I accompanied Ken to bars, and, although I was under age, nobody ever objected. Not on account of my size or looks, but on account of my certainty. Don't look back, he told me, don't doubt for a moment, just be surer of yourself than they are.

Once, another drinker started swearing at me – telling me to get my bloody mouth out of his sight – and I suddenly broke down. Ken put his arm round me and took me straight out into the street. There were no lights. This was in wartime London. We walked a long way in silence. If you have to cry, he said, and sometimes you can't help it, if you have to cry, cry afterwards, never during! Remember this. Unless you're with those who love you, only those who love you, and in that case you're already lucky for there are never many who love you – if you're with them, you can cry during. Otherwise you cry afterwards.

All the games he taught me, he played well. Except for his short-sightedness (suddenly it occurs to me, as I write, that all the people I have loved and still love were or are short-sighted), except for his short-sightedness, he moved like an athlete. A similar poise.

Not me. I was clumsy, over-hasty, cowardly, with almost no poise. I had something else though. A kind of determination, which, given my age, was startling. I would wager all! And for the energy of that rashness, he overlooked the rest. And the gift of his love was the gift of sharing with me what he knew, almost everything he knew, irrespective of my age or his.

For such a gift to be possible the giver and receiver need to be equal, and we, strange incongruous pair that we were, became equal. Probably neither of us understood how this happened. Now we do. We were foreseeing this moment; we were equal then as we are equal now in the Place Nowy. We foresaw my being an old man and his being dead, and this allowed us to be equal.

He puts his long hand around the can of beer on the table and clinks it against mine.

Whenever possible, he preferred gestures to spoken words. Perhaps as a result of his respect for silent written words. He must have studied in libraries, yet for him the immediate place for a book was a raincoat pocket. And the books he pulled out of that pocket!

He did not hand them to me directly. He said the name of the author, he pronounced the title and he placed the book on the corner of the mantelpiece in his bed-sitting room. Sometimes there were several, one on top of the other, so that I might choose. George Orwell. *Down and Out in Paris and London*. Marcel Proust. *Swann's Way*. Katherine Mansfield. *The Garden Party*. Laurence Sterne. *The Life and Opinions of Tristam Shandy*. Henry Miller. *Tropic of Cancer*. Neither of us, for different reasons, believed in literary explanations. I never once asked him about what I failed to understand. He never referred to what, given my age and experience, I might find difficult to grasp in these books. Sir Frederick Treves. *The Elephant Man and Other Reminiscences*. James Joyce. *Ulysses*. (An English edition published in Paris.) There was a tacit understanding between us that we learn – or try to learn – how to live partly from books. The learning begins with looking at our first illustrated alphabet, and goes on until we die. Oscar Wilde. *De Profundis*. St John of the Cross.

When I gave a book back, I felt closer to him, because I knew a little more of what he had read during his long life. Books converged us. Often one book lead to another. After George Orwell's *Down and Out in Paris and London*, I wanted to read *Homage to Catalonia*.

Ken was the first person to talk to me about the Spanish Civil War. Open wounds, he said. Nothing can staunch them. I had never heard the word *staunch* pronounced out loud before. We were at that moment playing billiards in a bar. Don't forget to chalk the cue, he added.

He read to me in Spanish a poem by García Lorca, who had been shot four years earlier, and when he translated it, I believed in my fourteen-year-old mind that I knew – except for a few details – what life was about and what had to be risked! Perhaps I told him so, or perhaps some other rashness of mine provoked him, for I remember him saying: Check out the details! Check them out first not last!

He said this with a note of regret as if somewhere, somehow, he himself had made a mistake about details that he regretted. No, I'm wrong. He was a man who regretted nothing. A mistake for which he had had to pay the price. During his life he paid the price for many things he didn't regret.

Two girls in long white lace dresses are crossing the far end of the Place Nowy. Ten or eleven years old, both tall for their age, both become Honorary Women, both, as they cross the square, stepping out of their childhood.

La Semaine blanche, Ken says. Last Sunday kids across the whole of Poland took their First Communion. And every day this week they do their best to get to a church and take communion once more, particularly the girls, the boys too but they are less noticeable and there are fewer of them, particularly the girls, who want to step out in their white communion dresses once again.

The two girls in the square walk side by side so they can scythe down the glances they are attracting.

They're going to the Church of Corpus Christi where

there's a famous Madonna in gold leaf, Ken says. All the girls of Kraków would like to take their First Communion in Corpus Christi because the communion dresses their mothers buy there are better cut, have a better length.

It was in the Old Met Music Hall on the Edgware Road, sitting beside him, that I first learnt how to judge claims to style, learnt the rudiments of criticism. Ruskin, Lukács, Berenson, Benjamin, Wolflin, all came later. My essential formation was in the Old Met, looking down from the gallery on to the triangular stage, surrounded by a noisily receptive and unforgiving public, who judged the stand-up comics, the adagio acrobats, the singers, the ventriloquists, pitilessly. We saw Tessa O'Shea bring the house down, and we saw her booed off stage, her hair wet with tears.

An act had to have style. The audience had to be won over twice a night. And to do this, the non-stop sequence of gags had to lead to something more mysterious: the conspiratorial, irreverent proposition that life itself was a stand-up act!

Max Miller, 'The Cheeky Chappie' in a silver suit with his hyperthyroid eyes, played on the triangular stage like an irrepressible sea lion, for whom every laugh was a fish to be swallowed.

I've got my own studios in Brighton, and a woman came to my house on Monday morning – she said, 'Max, I want you to paint a snake on my knee.' I went dead white, honest I did. No, well I'm not strong, I'm not strong. So, listen – I jumped out of bed, see . . . no, listen a minute . . . so I started to paint the snake just above her knee, that's where I started. But I had to chuck it – she smacked me in the face – I didn't know a snake was so long – how long's an ordinary snake?

Each comedian played a victim, a victim who had to win the hearts of all those who had bought tickets, and who were also victims.

Harry Champion came downstage, hands out, begging for help, on the verge of tragedy: 'Life is a very hard thing – you never come out of it alive!' When he said this on a good night, the whole house put itself in the palm of his hand.

Flanagan and Allen rushed on, as if on urgent business and late. Then they showed, at high speed, that the whole world and its urgencies was based on a profound misunderstanding. They were young. Flanagan had soulful, naive eyes; Ches Allen, the straight one, was dapper and correct. Yet together they demonstrated the decrepitude of the world!

If I could sell my taxi I'd go back to Africa and do what I used to do.

What's that?

Dig holes and sell them to farmers!

The microphone is going to kill their art, Ken whispered to me in the gallery. I asked him what he meant. Listen to how they use their voices, he explained. They talk across the whole theatre and we're in the middle of them. If they use a mike, this will stop and the public will no longer be in the middle. The secret of music hall artists is that they play defenceless, like we all are. A player with a mike is armed! It's another ball game.

He was right. The music hall died during the next decade.

A woman, carrying a basket of wild sorrel, passes the table in the Place Nowy.

Could you make us some sorrel soup? Ken asks me. We could have it tomorrow instead of borsch.

I guess so.

With eggs?

That I've never tried.

Well, he shuts his eyes, you prepare the soup, serve it, and in each bowl, you put a hot hard-boiled egg. You have made sure that beside each bowl there's a knife as well as a spoon. You cut the egg into slices, and you eat it with the green soup. And the mixture of the sharp green acidity and the round comfort of the egg reminds you of something extraordinary and far away.

Of home?

Certainly not, not even for the Poles.

Of what then?

Of survival, perhaps.

It seemed to me that Ken always lived in the same bedsit. In reality, he moved often, but the moves were made when I was away at school and on returning and going to see him, I would find his same few possessions piled up on a similar table at the foot of a similar bed, behind a door with a key, which opened on to a staircase, overlooked by a landlady, worrying in the same way about the lights being left on.

Ken's room had a gas fire and a tall window. On the mantelpiece above the gas fire he stacked our books. On the table by the window was a large portable wireless (the word radio was rarely used) to which we listened. 2 Sept. 1939: the Panzer divisions of the Wehrmacht invaded Poland without warning this morning at dawn. Six million Poles, half of them Jewish, were going to lose their lives during the next five years.

In the room's wardrobe he kept not only clothes but food: oatmeal biscuits, hard-boiled eggs, a pineapple, coffee. Attached to the gas fire was a gas ring for heating water in a saucepan that he kept on the windowsill. The room smelt of cigarettes, pineapple, and lighter fuel. The toilet and washbasin were on the landing either above or below. I tended to forget which, and he would shout after me: Up not Down!

His two suitcases, which he left open on the floor, were never entirely unpacked. At that time nothing was unpacked, even in people's heads. Everything was in store or in transit. Dreams were kept on luggage racks, in kitbags and in suitcases. In one of the cases open on the floor there was a jar of honey from Brittany, a dark fisherman's sweater, a volume of Baudelaire in French, and a table-tennis bat.

Give you a lead of fifteen plus service! he proposed. Ready? Serve! Fifteen, love. Fifteen, one. Fifteen, two. Fifteen, three. He was beating me like that in 1940.

By 1941 he was still beating me two games out of three, but he was no longer giving me a lead.

He was now working in some capacity, about which he would say nothing, for a foreign service at the BBC. He often came back to the room after work in the small hours of the morning. The bedcover was damasked.

In the mornings we usually took breakfast in a barricaded café near Gloucester Road. Food was rationed. Those without a sweet tooth gave their sugar rations to others. Ken and I drank tea, as it was better than the coffee essence. Over breakfast we read newspapers. Each consisted of four – or at the most six – pages. 9 Sept. 1941: Leningrad cut off by German troops. 12 Feb. 1942: Three German cruisers sail unimpeded through the Straits of Dover. 25 May 1942: The Wehrmacht take 250,000 Soviet prisoners at Kharkov. The Nazis, Ken said, are making the same mistake as Napoleon: they underestimate the power of General Winter. He was right. In late November General Paulus and his 6th Army were surrounded at Stalingrad and in February they surrendered to General Zhukov.

One morning in the middle of April 1943, Ken told me about a London radio broadcast, made the day before, by General Sikorski, the Polish prime minister in exile, who was appealing to Poles in Poland to support the ongoing uprising in the Warsaw ghetto. The ghetto was being systematically annihilated. Sikorski said – Ken spoke slowly – that: 'The greatest crime in the history of mankind is taking place.'

Only during moments of forgetfulness, when thinking about nothing, did the enormity of what was happening make itself felt. The enormity was then present in the air, under the spring sky, addressing a seventh sense which I still cannot name.

11 July 1943. The British 8th Army and the American 7th Army invade Sicily and take Syracuse.

I think of you as a beginner, Ken whispers, leaning across the table in Kraków, and I suspect that if I read you today I might be disappointed.

About mastery there is something sad, indescribably sad, I reply.

I see you as a beginner.

Still?

More than ever!

With you as teacher?

I didn't teach. You learnt. There's a difference. I let you learn! And there were a few things I learnt from you!

Such as?

Dressing quickly.

Anything else?

How to read well out loud.

You read well out loud yourself, I say.

In the end I discovered how you did it. The secret of your reading out loud. You didn't read the end of the sentence until you got there, that was your secret. You refused to look ahead.

He takes off his glasses as if he has seen and said enough. He knew me well.

Beneath the damasked bedcover, during nights punctuated by air-raid sirens, I sometimes felt a burning in Ken's erect member. The tumescence came unasked and waited like a pain, a pain that had to be staunched, low down in the middle of his long body. Soon afterwards, in the bed damp with spunk and tears from his eyes without glasses, sleep came swiftly to the two of us. Rippled sleep, like sand when the tide is far out.

Let's go and see the pigeons, Ken says, polishing the thick lenses of his glasses with his tartan handkerchief.

We walk towards the northern end of the market. The sun is hot. One more early summer morning added to the pile on the century's desk. We watch two butterflies who came to the centre of the city with the garden vegetables fly upwards in a spiral. The clock on the city cathedral strikes eleven.

Every day, hundreds of Polish visitors climb the spiral stone staircase in the bell tower of the cathedral to look across the Vistula and to touch with a finger the massive tongue of the Zygmunt bell, cast in 1520 and weighing eleven tons. Touching it is said to bring luck in love.

We pass a man selling hairdryers. One hundred and fifty złoty each, which means they have probably been stolen. He is demonstrating one of the dryers and calls out to a passing child: Come here, sweetie, and I'll make you cool! The girl laughs, agrees and her hair fluffs up, billowing. *Slicznie*, she cries.

I'm beautiful, Ken translates, laughing.

Further on I see a crowd of men huddled together. If it weren't for their craning heads and the silence in the air, I would say they were listening to music. When we get closer I understand that they are in fact gathered round a table on which there are a hundred pigeons in wooden pens, five or six to a cage. The birds vary in plumage and size, although all have a glint of bluish slate in their colouring, and in this glint there is something of the sky above Kraków. The pigeons on the table look like sky-samples brought back to earth. Maybe this is why the men seemed to be listening to music.

Nobody knows, Ken says, how homing pigeons find their way home. When they are flying in clear weather, they can see thirty kilometres ahead, yet this doesn't explain their unerring sense of direction. During the siege of Paris in 1870, a million messages to the city's inhabitants were delivered by fifty pigeons. It was the first time that micro-photography had ever been used on that sort of scale. The letters were all reduced, so that hundreds could fit on a tiny film weighing only a gram or two. Then, when the pigeons arrived, the letters were enlarged, copied out and distributed. Strange how things come together in history – colodium film and carrier pigeons!

Some birds have been taken out of their cages and are being expertly examined by the pigeon fanciers. Their crops are being lightly pinched between two fingers, the length of their legs measured, the flat tops of their heads gently pressed by a thumb, their flight feathers extended, and all the while they are being held close against the men's chests, like trophies.

It's hard, don't you think, says Ken taking my arm, to imagine sending news of a total catastrophe by carrier pigeon? The message could announce a defeat, or it could be an appeal for help, but in that gesture of throwing the pigeon up into the sky, so that it heads for home, isn't there inevitably some hope? Sailors from Ancient Egypt used to release pigeons from their boats on the high seas to tell their families they were on their way home.

I look at the beady red-pupilled eyes of one of the pigeons. He is looking at nothing, because he knows he's held and can't move.

I wonder how the chess game is going, I say. The two of us stroll to the other end of the market.

There are sixteen pieces left on the board. Zedrek has king, bishop and five pawns. He is looking up at the sky as if seeking inspiration. Abram looks at his watch. Twenty-three minutes! he announces.

Chess is not a game you can hurry, comments a customer.

He has one good move, whispers Ken, and I bet he's not going to see it.

Move the bishop to C5, is that it?

No, you idiot, his king to F1.

Tell him then.

Dead men don't move pieces!

Hearing Ken say these words I suffer his death. He,

98

meanwhile, takes his head in his hands, and with them he turns the head left and right, as if it were a searchlight. He waits for me to laugh as I often did at this clown act of his. He doesn't see my anguish. I do laugh.

When I came out of the army at the end of the war, he had disappeared. I wrote to him at the last address I had, and there was no reply. A year later he sent a postcard to my parents – the postcard came from somewhere improbable like Iceland or Jersey – asking whether we might all spend Christmas together, which we did. He came with a woman war-photographer who was, I think, Czech. We played Christmas games, we laughed a lot, he teased my mother about buying all the food on the black market.

Between the two of us there was the same complicity. Neither of us looked away or took the slightest step back. We felt the same love: simply the circumstances had changed. The *passeur* had delivered his charge; the frontiers were crossed.

The years passed. The last time I ever saw him we drove all night with my friend Anant from London to Genève. Driving through a forest near Châtillon-sur-Seine we heard Coltrane on the radio playing 'My Favourite Things'. It was during this journey that Ken told me he was returning to New Zealand. He was then sixty-five. I didn't ask him why because I didn't want to hear him say: To die.

Instead I made believe that he would come back to Europe. To which he replied: The best thing there, John, down under, is the grass! There's no grass as green anywhere else in the world. He said this forty years ago. I never knew exactly when or how he died.

In the Place Nowy, among the stolen hairdryers, the honey-bread with its candied orange peel, the woman who chain-smokes and hopes to sell dresses, Jagusia with her basket now almost empty, the black cherries that have to be sold and eaten quickly because they won't last, the barrel of salted herring, the voice of Ewa Demarczyk on a CD, singing one of her defiant songs, I suffer his death for the first time.

I do not even glance at where Ken is standing, for he will not be there. I walk alone, past the barber's, past the soup kitchen, past the women sitting on their stools.

Something pulls me back to the pigeons. When I arrive a man turns towards me, and, as if guessing at my distress – is there another country in the world more accustomed to coming to terms with that emotion? – he hands me, without smiling, the carrier pigeon he is holding.

Its feathers feel slightly damp – like satin. The small ones on its breast have a parting in the middle, as on an owl. It weighs nothing for its size. I hold him against my chest.

I left the Place Nowy, and found, after asking two passers-by, the bankomat. From there I returned to the pension in Miodowa Street and lay down on the bed. It was very hot, hot with the uncertain heat of the eastern plains. Now I could weep. Later I shut my eyes and imagined shuffling a pack of cards.

4

Some Fruit as Remembered by the Dead

Melon

Melons seemed to us to be, by a kind of negation, the fruit of drought. Walking through parched valleys, or over the cracked earth of dusty plains, we came upon melons and we ate them as you might draw water from a well in an oasis. They were improbable, they comforted us, but in fact they did not really quench our thirst. Even before they are open, melons smell of a sweet enclosed water. A heavy enclosing smell with no edges to it. Whereas to quench your thirst you need something sharp. Lemons are better.

When small and green, a melon may suggest youth. But quickly the fruit becomes oddly ageless – like a mother to her child. The blemishes on its skin – and there are always some – are like moles or birthmarks. They do not imply ageing as blemishes do on other fruit. They simply confirm that this unique melon is and was always itself.

To somebody who had never eaten one, its exterior would give little idea of what to expect within. The flagrant orange, never seen till the moment of opening, veering toward green. The abundant seeds lying in the central hollow, the colour of pale flames but wet, their placing and clustering defying any clear sense of order. And everywhere the glistening.

The taste of the melon included both darkness and sunshine. It miraculously united these opposites, which can otherwise never exist together.

Peach

Our peaches blackened in the sun. A crimson-black to be sure, but with more black in it than red: black like iron which has been heated red-hot and has been slaked and is cooling and gives no warning of the heat it still holds. The peach of the horseshoes.

The black seldom extended over the entire surface. There were parts which, when the fruit was on the tree, were in shadow, and these were whitish, although in the white there was a touch of green, as if the leaves that cast the shadow had just brushed the skin with a finger of their own colour.

In our time, rich European women took enormous pains to keep their faces and bodies as pale as that colour. But never the gypsies.

The size of the peaches varied considerably, from ones large enough to fill the hand, to small ones no bigger than billiard balls. The skin of the smaller ones, being finer, had a tendency to wrinkle very slightly when the fruit was bruised or overripe.

Those wrinkles often reminded us of warm skin in the fold of a dark arm.

In the centre you found a stone, with the texture of a dark bark and an aspect as sulphurous as a meteorite.

These wild peaches were the fruit made by God for thieves.

Greengages

We looked for greengages every year during the month of August. Frequently they disappointed. Either they were unripe, fibrous, almost dry, or else they were over-soft and mushy. Many were not worth biting into, for one could feel with one's finger that they did not have the right temperature: a temperature unfindable in Celsius or Fahrenheit: the temperature of a particular coolness surrounded by sunshine. The temperature of a small boy's fist.

The boy is somewhere between eight and ten-and-a-half years old, the age of independence, before the press of adolescence. The boy holds the greengage in his hand, brings it to his mouth, bites, and the fruit darts its tongue against the back of his throat so that he swallows its promise.

A promise of what? Of something that has not yet been named and he will soon name. He tastes a sweetness which no longer has anything to do with sugar, but with a limb which goes on and on, and seems to have no end. The limb belongs to a body which he can only see with his eyes shut. The body has three more limbs and a neck and ankles and is like his own; except that it is inside out. Through the limb without end flows a sap – he can taste it between his teeth – the sap of a nameless pale wood, which he calls girl-tree.

It was enough that one greengage in a hundred reminded us of that.

Cherries

In cherries, there was the flavour of fermentation as in no other fruit. Picked straight from the tree, they tasted of enzymes laced with the sun and this taste was complementary with the special shiny polish of their skins.

Eat cherries – even one hour after they have been picked – and their taste blends with that of their own rottenness. In the gold or red of their colour there is always a hint of brown: the colour into which they will soften and disintegrate.

The cherry refreshes, not on account of its purity – as does the apple – but by slightly, almost imperceptibly, tickling the tongue with the effervescence of its fermenting.

Because of the small size of the cherry and the lightness of its flesh and the insubstantiality of its skin, the cherry stone was always incongruous. The eating of the cherry never quite prepared you for its stone. When you spat it out, it seemed to have little connection with the flesh that surrounded it. It felt more like a precipitate of your own body, a precipitate mysteriously produced by the act of eating cherries. After each cherry, you spat out a cherry tooth.

Lips, as distinct from the rest of the face, have the same gloss as cherries do and the same malleability. Both their skins are like the skin of a liquid. A question of their capillary surfaces. Make a test to see whether our memory is correct or whether the dead exaggerate. Put a cherry in your mouth, don't bite it yet, now for a split second remark how the density, the softness and the resilence of the fruit match perfectly the nature of your lips which hold it.

Quetsch

A dark, small, oval plum, not much longer than a human eye. When they are ripe in September on the tree, they glance between the leaves. Quetsches.

Ripe, their colour is a blackish-purple, but their skin, unless when handling it you rub it off with your fingers, has a bloom on it: a bloom the colour of blue wood-smoke. These two colours made us think of drowning and flying at the same time.

Their pale yellowy-green flesh is both sweetish and astringent, so that its taste is a serrated one – like the blade of a minute saw along which you gently run your tongue. The quetsch doesn't seduce as the greengage does.

The trees were always planted near the house. During the winter, looking out through the window, we saw each day small birds searching for food and assembling and perching on the branches. Finches, robins, tits, sparrows and an occasional poaching magpie. In the spring, before the blossom flowered, the same small birds would sing in the quetsch tree.

There is another reason why they are the fruit of song. From barrels full of quetsch, when the fruit were fermented, we distilled illegal *gnôle*, plum brandy, *slivovitz*. And sparkling little glasses of this invariably prompted us to sing songs of love, solitude and endurance.

5

Islington

The borough of Islington has, during the last twenty-five years, become fashionable. In the fifties and sixties, the name Islington, when pronounced in central London or in the north-western suburbs, conjured up a remote and faintly suspect district. It is interesting to note how poor and therefore uneasy districts, even when they are geographically near a city centre, are pushed, in the imagination of those who are prospering, further away than they really are. Harlem in New York is an obvious example. For Londoners today Islington is far closer than it used to be.

When it was still remote, forty years ago, Hubert bought a small terraced house there, with a narrow back garden that sloped down to a canal. At that time he and his wife were teaching part-time in art schools and had no money to spare. The house, however, was cheap, dirt cheap.

They've moved to Islington! a friend told me at the time. And this news was like a late autumn afternoon when the daylight hours are becoming noticeably shorter. There was something of a foreclosure about it.

Soon afterwards, I went to live abroad. Occasionally over the years and on visits to London, I saw Hubert at the house of a common friend, but I never visited – until three days ago – his house in Islington. He and I had been students together at the same London art school in 1943. He was studying Textile Design and I was studying Painting, but there were certain classes we attended together: Life Drawing, History of Architecture, Human Anatomy.

He made an impression on me because of his fastidious persistence. He invariably wore a tie. He looked like a nineteenth-century bookbinder. He tended to be in a state of sad shock provoked by recurring modern stupidities, and his nails were always clean. I wore a long black Romantic overcoat and looked like a coachman – also of the nineteenth century. I drew with the blackest charcoal I could find, and to find any at all during the war wasn't easy – who had time in '41 or '42 to be burning charcoal? Sometimes I filched a stick from the teacher's supply; two kinds of theft were justifiable: Food for the hungry, Basic Materials for the artist.

The two of us were undoubtedly suspicious of one another. Hubert must have thought I was over-demonstrative and indiscreet to the point of exhibitionism; he seemed to me to be a tight-lipped elitist.

Nevertheless we listened to one another and would sometimes drink a beer together or share an apple. We were both aware that we were each considered by most of the other students to be deranged. Deranged because of our commitment to working at every possible moment. Practically nothing distracted us. Hubert drew from the model with the attentive restrained movements of a violinist tuning his instrument; I drew like a kitchen boy slapping tomatoes and cheese on to pizzas waiting to be put into the oven. Our approaches were very different. Nevertheless during the breaks every hour, when the model took a rest, we were the only two who stayed in the studio and went on working. Hubert often improved his drawing, bringing it to a kind of equanimity. I usually ruined mine.

Three days ago, after I had rung the bell of the house in Islington, he came to the front door with a beaming smile. His left arm was raised above his head in a gesture which was something between a welcome, a salute, and a cavalry officer's sign to his men to advance. Nobody could be less military than Hubert. Nevertheless he is a commander.

His face was gaunt and so meticulously shaved it looked sore. He was wearing a pair of baggy corduroy trousers with a wide black leather belt that hung loose, almost at the level of his trouser pockets.

Perfect timing, he said, the water has just boiled. Whereupon he waited for me to make some remark.

It's been a long time, I said.

By now we were at the top of the first short flight of stairs.

What kind of tea would you prefer: Earl Grey, Darjeeling or Green Leaf?

Green Leaf.

It's the healthiest, he said, it's what I drink every day.

The drawing room was full of rugs, cushions, objects, footrests, porcelain, dried flowers, collections, engravings, crystal decanters, pictures. It was hard to imagine anything new, anything new larger than a postcard, finding a home there, for there was no space. It was equally hard to imagine throwing a piece out to make more space, for everything had been found and chosen and placed over the years with the same love and attention. There was not a sea shell, a candlestick, a clock, a stool that stood out or appeared awkward. He indicated that I should sit in a Regency chair by the fireplace.

I enquired who had painted an abstract watercolour hanging near the door.

That's one of Gwen's, Hubert said. I've always liked it.

Gwen, his wife, a teacher of engraving, died twelve years ago. She was withdrawn, small, wore brogue shoes and looked like a lepidopterist. If she had held up her hand in the air anywhere – even on a wartime London bus – I would have expected a butterfly to land on it.

Hubert poured from a silver teapot into a Derbyshire cup on a table by the door and navigated around the many pieces of furniture across the room to deliver it to me. I wondered whether for him each room in the house had a navigation chart, like seas do. On the ground floor I had noticed the dining room was equally encumbered.

I made some cucumber sandwiches, if you would like one? he asked.

Thank you very much.

I had an aunt, he said, who maintained there were two golden rules about invitations to tea. One is that cucumber sandwiches and sponge cake are obligatory items, and the second is that guests have to insist upon leaving, and succeed in doing so, before six o'clock . . .

I heard the ticking of a pendulum clock on the shelf behind me. There were at least four clocks in the room.

I want to ask you a question about our art-school days, I said. Do you remember a girl, the same year as us, who was studying Theatre Costume? She went around a lot with Colette.

Colette! replied Hubert, I wonder what has become of her? She used to come in with a new dress every week, remember? Often with the pins still in it.

She used to stay with Colette in her rooms in Guildford Place, I said. The rooms were on the first floor, over-looking Coram's Fields. She was short, snub-nosed, had large eyes, was a little plump. Not at all talkative.

Coram's Fields, said Hubert. I saw a painting of them in a show the other day. By a young painter called Arturo di Stefano. Kids on a hot, hot day by a swimming pool playing with the water. Full of the eternity – if I may so put it – of childhood!

No swimming pool there then, I said. Just a boarded-up bandstand, and the tall trees that looked down at us in the morning when we looked out of the window.

I don't think I was ever at Colette's place, Hubert said.

Do you see whom I'm thinking about though?

Was it Pauline who had an affair with Joe, the framer?

No, no, dark hair, short dark hair! Very white teeth. A bit stand-offish, walked around with her nose in the air.

You're not thinking of Jeanne with the two n's to her name?

Jeanne was tall! This one was small, roundish, tiny. She used to go home for weekends to somewhere smart like Newbury. Was it Newbury? Anyway, she loved horses.

Why do you need to know her name?

I've been trying for a long time to remember her name, and it keeps escaping me.

Was it Priscilla?

It was a very common name, that's what's so strange.

Probably she got married, most art students got married in those days and then her family name would have changed.

I only want her first name.

Are you trying to trace her whereabouts today?

On Mondays in June she came with strawberries from the countryside and would hand them round the whole class.

She may be dead, don't forget!

There are only a few people today whom I can consult, that's why I came to you.

True, unfortunately true. We are not so many. What was her work like?

Dull. Yet as soon as she came into a room you knew she had a sense of style. She shone. She said nothing and she shone.

I've always maintained that style is the inheritance of a

number of talents. A single talent, however great, does not yield a sense of style. Did I take one of my pills? I'm talking too much.

I didn't see you do so.

I wish I could place her for you. I'm afraid I can't. She's gone.

Nobody wore hats in those days, and she did! She wore a hat as if she was going to the races! Askew on the back of her head.

He said nothing. I let him think. And the silence continued. Hubert had always been prone to silences — as if life hung by a thread and foolish talking might snap it. In the silence I could feel that, since Gwen's death, the standards the two of them had established and maintained here had in no way changed. What this room *liked* was still the same.

Let's go upstairs, he finally said, and I'll show you St Paul's, a splendid view of St Paul's from the balcony of my bedroom.

We took the stairs slowly. He held himself very upright. On the first landing he stopped and said: This terrace was built in the 1840s and the houses were destined for clerks who worked in the City. Poor man's Georgian, as you can see. And it didn't work out. Within a generation they had all been turned into lodging houses, with one or a couple of tenants living on each floor. And so it remained for a hundred years. When we arrived, forty years ago, the houses on the other side of the street didn't even have electricity. Only gas and paraffin lamps.

The wall of the staircase we were climbing was hung with sketches for textiles and framed samples of precious fabrics, some of them Persian-looking.

Before we bought this house it was a brothel, serving the lorry drivers who delivered goods to London from the North. Come into the bathroom. See that mirror with the mermaids? The tenants left it in the bedroom downstairs and Gwen insisted upon keeping it. Sometimes I see Beatrice in it, Gwen would say laughing, Beatrice waving at me! Beatrice was a whore and her name is scratched on one of the window panes in the drawing room.

As Hubert straightened the mirror on the bathroom wall, I caught a glimpse of his face in the glass and was reminded of him as a young man. Perhaps something to do with the glass being speckled and darkened, so that the expression in his eyes was by contrast more sparkling.

When we moved in we had no money, so we told ourselves it might take as long to make a house as it takes to make a garden. We restored it room by room, there are seven, floor by floor, year by year.

On the top floor Hubert led me across his bedroom towards the French windows which gave on to a terrace.

Mind the geraniums! he said. I keep them out here to water them every morning.

They smell so strong!

Bloody cranesbill, he said, or in Latin: *Geranium sanguineum*.

I picked one of the leaves and sniffed it. It reminded me of her hair.

During the war ordinary soap was scarce, and there were no shampoos, unless you bought them on the black market. So newly washed hair smelt of itself. I remember her washing her hair in the morning after getting out of bed. It was summer and warm, and the windows were open. She washed it in an enamel handbasin which she filled with water from an enamel jug. There was no hot water in Colette's flat. Then she came back, with a towel wrapped round her head and nothing else on, lay down on the bed beside me and waited until her hair dried.

St Paul's, Hubert said, there's nothing else to match it! And built in record time, only thirty-five years! Work began nine years after the Great Fire of London in 1666, and it was finished in 1710. Christopher Wren was still around to see his masterpiece inaugurated.

He was reciting, almost word for word, what we had been obliged to learn by heart in the History of Architecture class. We were also obliged to go and draw the cathedral. It had survived many air raids unscathed, and had become a great patriotic monument. Churchill was filmed speaking in front of it. And when I drew its architectural details, I added Spitfire fighters in the sky behind!

The first time it was neither she nor I who made a choice. I had come to visit Colette after an evening class. We ate some soup. The three of us talked and it grew late. There was an air-raid warning. We switched off the lights and opened a window to watch the searchlights raking the sky above the trees in Coram's Fields. The raiders didn't seem especially near.

Sleep here, Colette proposed. It's better than going out. We can all sleep in this bed, it's large enough for four.

Which is what we did. Colette slept against the wall, she in the middle, and I on the outside. We took off most of our clothes but not all.

When we woke up, Colette was making toast and pouring cups of tea, and she and I were entangled together, legs and arms interlaced. We were not surprised by this, for both of us were aware of something more surprising: during the night each of us had put to sleep the other's sex, not by satisfying it, or by denying it, but by following a different desire which even today it's hard to name. No clinical descriptions fit. Perhaps it could only have happened in London during the spring of 1943. We found in each other's arms a way of leaving together, a transport elsewhere. We arranged ourselves, fitted ourselves together as if we were making a sleigh or a skateboard. (Only skateboards didn't yet exist.) Our destination wasn't important. Any departure was to an erogenous zone. What mattered was the distance we put behind us. We fed each other distance with every lick. Wherever our skins touched there was the promise of an horizon.

I stepped back into Hubert's bedroom, and noticed that it was different from the rest of the house. There was a double bed in the corner, but Gwen had never slept up here. This room was provisional – as though during the last decade Hubert had been camping here. The walls were entirely covered with images of plants and flowers – unframed prints, drawings, photographs, pages torn from books – and they were placed so close together that they looked almost like a wallpaper. Many were attached by drawing pins, and they made me think that he was constantly rearranging them. Except for the slippers under the bed and the collection of medicines on the bedside table, it looked like a student's room.

He noticed my interest and he pointed to a drawing, perhaps one of his own: Strange flower, no? Like the breast of a tiny thrush in full song! It originally came from Brazil. In English it's known as Birthwort. In Latin: *Aristolochia elegans*. Somewhere Lévi-Strauss says something about the Latin name of a plant. He says the Latin name personalises it. Birthwort is merely a species. *Aristolochia elegans* is a person, singular and unique. If you had this flower in your garden and it happened to die, you could mourn for it with its Latin name. Which you wouldn't do, if you knew it as Birthwort.

I was standing by the French windows. Shall I shut them? I asked.

Yes, do.

You always sleep with the windows shut?

Funny you should ask that, for recently it has been something of a problem. Before it was simple – I left them open all night. Now, before I go to bed, I open them. The house is so narrow it tends to be stuffy as soon as all the windows are shut. The other night I thought of the clerks who lived here when the house was new. Compared to us, they had very little space in their lives. Cramped offices, cramped horse-buses, cramped streets, cramped rooms. Then, come the small hours, before it's light, I get out of bed again and I go and shut the windows, so that when the street wakes up in the morning it's quiet.

You sleep late?

I wake up early, very early. I think I shut the windows because I need a kind of protection at the beginning of each new day. For some time now I've needed calm in the morning so I can face it. Every day you have to decide to be invincible.

I understand.

I doubt it, John. I'm a solitary man. Come, I'll show you the garden.

I had never before seen a garden like this one. It was full of bushes, flowers, shrubs, each flourishing, yet planted so close together it was impossible for a stranger to imagine finding a way between them. A single path led down to the canal and it was so tight one could only go down it walking sideways. Yet the density of the foliage was not like that of a jungle, but like the density of a closed book, which has to be read page by page. I spotted Michaelmas daisies, Winter jasmine, Powder-puff holly-hocks and, bordering the path, Ribbon Grass known as Lady's Laces, and a citronella plant whose leaves, shaped like tongues, were growing in such a way, and had placed themselves in such an arrangement, that each was accommodated within the other's space. Each had found a position beside, or under, or over, or between, or around, its neighbouring leaves that allowed it to receive some light, to bend with the wind, to probe in its natural direction. And the whole impenetrable garden was like this.

There was nothing here when we came, said Hubert, not even grass. It had been used for years as a dump for all the houses along the terrace. A dump behind the brothel. Old baths, a gas stove, smashed prams, rotten rabbit-hutches. Try some of these grapes.

He stepped up to a vine growing against a brick wall that separated the garden from the neighbour's. Over each bunch of grapes he had placed a plastic bag to prevent the birds from eating them. He inserted his long hand inside one of these bags and, with his fingers, detached a few small white grapes, the colour of cloudy honey, and placed them on the palm of my hand.

The next time I went to Colette's flat in Guildford Place it was understood from the start that I would spend the night there. Colette slept on another bed in the second room. I took off all my clothes and she put on her loose embroidered nightdress. We discovered the same thing as last time. Once put together, we could leave. We travelled from bone to bone, from continent to continent. Sometimes we spoke. Not sentences, not endearments. The names of parts and places. Tibia and Timbuktu, Labia and Lapland, Earhole and Oasis. The names of the parts became pet names, the names of the places, passwords. We weren't dreaming. We simply became the Vasco da

Gama of our two bodies. We paid the closest attention to each other's sleep, we never forgot one another. When she was deeply asleep her breathing was like surf. You took me to the bottom, she told me one morning.

We did not become lovers, we were scarcely friends, and we had little in common. I was not interested in horses, and she wasn't interested in the Freedom Press. When our paths crossed in the art school we had nothing to say to each other. This didn't worry us. We exchanged light kisses – on the shoulder or the back of the neck, never on the mouth – and we continued on our separate ways, like an elderly couple who happened to be working in the same school. As soon as it became dark, whenever we could, we met to do the same thing: to pass the whole night in each other's arms and, like this, to leave, to go elsewhere. Repeatedly.

Hubert was attaching an armful of stems with yellow flowers to a trellis with several lengths of raffia, his hands still trembling a little.

It's getting chilly, he said, let's go inside.

He shut and locked the door behind us.

This is my workroom – he nodded towards a large wooden bench with a chair in front of it – this week I'm putting seeds from the garden into little packets, each one properly labelled with its common and Latin names. Occasionally I have to look the Latin one up in the herbarium, my memory isn't what it was, though I'm happy to say I don't have to do it often.

What are these packets for? I asked.

I send them away. Every autumn I do the same. See these here. Love-in-a-mist. *Nigella damascena*. Two dozen packets.

You mean you sell them?

I give them away.

So many! You've got hundreds of packets!

There's an organisation which calls itself 'Thrive', and they distribute seeds to people in need – old people's homes, orphanages, reception centres, transit camps – so that there are flowers in places where usually there would be none. It doesn't make much difference, of course, I realise that, but at least it's something. And for me, now, it's a way of sharing the pleasures of the garden. It's a satisfaction.

My recidivist erections were at first a distraction but once she had named them – we'll call them London! she said – they took their place and became no more urgent than – or as urgent as – the damp fern smell of her sweat, her rounded knees, or the curly black hairs in her arse-hole. Everything under the blankets took us elsewhere. And elsewhere, we discovered the size of life. In daylight life often seemed small. For example, when drawing plaster casts of Roman statues in the Antique class, it seemed very small. Under the blankets she fingered the soles of my feet with her toes and sighed 'Damascus'. I combed her hair with my teeth and hissed 'Scalp'. Then as these or other gestures of ours became longer and slower and we succumbed to a single sleep, our two bodies took account of the unimaginable distances they offered one another and we left. In the morning we said nothing. We couldn't make sentences. Either she would go and wash her hair, or I would go to the window at the foot of the bed and look out across Coram's Fields and she would throw me my trousers.

My real problem, said Hubert, is in the drawers over there.

He pulled out a metal drawer which slid noiselessly towards us. Double imperial size, designed for storing architectural plans. The drawer was full of small abstract sketches and watercolours which gave the impression they were derived from places. Perhaps microscopic places, perhaps galactic. Paths. Localities. Openings. Obstacles. All drawn with fluid washes and meandering lines. Hubert gave the drawer a soft push and it slid back on its rails. He pulled out another – there were a dozen such drawers – which, this time, contained drawings. Intricately drawn with a hard pencil, full of scudding movements, such as you see in clouds and running water.

What am I to do with them? he asked.

They are Gwen's?

He nodded.

If I leave them here, he said, they'll be thrown away after my death. If I make a selection and keep only what seem to me to be the very best, what do I do with the others? Burn them? Give them to an art school or a library? They are not interested. When she was alive, Gwen never made a name for herself. She was simply passionate about drawing, about 'capturing it' as she put it. She drew almost every day. She herself threw a lot away. What's in these drawers is what she wanted to keep.

He pulled out a third drawer, hesitated, and then selected with his slightly trembling hand a gouache and held it up.

Beautiful, I said.

What am I to do? I keep on putting it off. And if I do nothing, they'll all be thrown out.

You must put them in envelopes, I said.

Envelopes?

Yes. You sort them. You invent any system you like. By year, by colour, by preference, by size, by mood. And on each of the big envelopes you write her name and the category you've established. It'll take time. Not a single one must be misplaced. And in each envelope you put the drawings in order; you write a number very lightly on the back of each one.

An order according to what?

I don't know. You'll find out. There are drawings which look as if they should come first, and there's always a last drawing, isn't there? The order will take care of itself.

And what difference do you think these envelopes are going to make?

Who can tell? In any case they'll be better off.

You mean the drawings?

Yes. They'll be better off.

The clocks in the drawing room upstairs were chiming.

I must be off, I said.

He led me towards the front door. And after opening it, turning round, he looked at me quizzically.

Wasn't her name Audrey?

Audrey! Of course it was Audrey!

Funny little thing she was, said Hubert. She left I think after a couple of terms, which is why I couldn't place her straight away. She wasn't with us for long. And she wore hats, you're right.

He smiled distantly, for he could see I was pleased. We said our goodbyes.

The nameless desire Audrey and I shared came to an end as inexplicably as it had begun: inexplicably only because neither of us sought an explanation. The last time we slept together (and although I forgot her name, I can remember without the slightest hesitation that it was the month of June and her feet were dusty from wearing sandals all day long) she got into bed first, and I climbed on to the windowsill to detach the wooden frame of the blackout curtain, so that I could open the window and let in more air. Outside there was moonlight and all the trees around Coram's Fields were distinctly visible. I took in their every detail with a pleasure which included an anticipation because, in a minute or two, we would both, before setting out on the night's journey, be touching every detail of the other's body.

I slithered into bed beside her, and without a word she turned her back on me. There are a hundred ways of turning the back in bed. Most are inviting, some are languid. There is a way, though, that unmistakably announces refusal. Her shoulder blades became like armour plate.

I missed her too much to go to sleep, and she, I guessed, was pretending to sleep. I might have argued with her or started to kiss the back of her neck. Yet this was not our style. Bit by bit my perplexity slipped away and I felt thankful. I turned my own back and lay there cradling a gratitude for all that had happened in the bed with broken springs. At this moment a bomb fell. It was close by; we heard the windows shattering on the other side of the Fields and, further away, shouts. Neither of us spoke. Her shoulder blades relaxed. Her hand looked for mine, and we both lay there grateful.

Next morning when I left she didn't so much as glance up from her coffee bowl. She was staring into it as if she had decided, a few minutes before, that this was what she must do and that the future of our two lives depended upon it.

Hubert stood there in the doorway, left arm raised about his head, making a sign for the mounted troops to disperse. His face was fragile and invincible. It was getting dark.

I'll take your tip about the envelopes, he called after me.

I walked alone down the road past the other terraced houses.

You called me many names in your sleep, Audrey said as she took my arm, and my favourite was Oslo.

127

Oslo! I repeated, as we turned into Upper Street. The way her head now rested on my shoulder told me she was dead.

You said it rhymed with First Snow, she said.

6

Le Pont d'Arc

Month of February. Slight frost at night. 21° C at midday. Cloudless sky above the village of Vogué on the east bank of the Ardèche. The sound of water flowing over, polishing, shifting stones. The river, full of swirls, fast-flowing, metallic-looking in the sunlight, is less than twenty metres wide. It tugs like a dog at the imagination, asking for you to come for a walk. A notoriously capricious river whose level can rise six metres in less than three hours. In it, I'm told, there are pike, but no *sandre*.

I watch the birds upstream as they dive across the silver surface. Earlier this morning I went to pray for Anne in the church under the limestone cliffs. She is the mother of my friend Simon and is dying in her house with a garden in Cambridge. If I could, I would have sent her the sound of the Ardèche with its unwavering yet imprecise promise.

The waters of the Ardèche have made many caves in the plateau of the Bas Vivarais and, from time immemorial, the caves have offered shelter to the intrepid.

On my way here I gave a lift to a man from Lyon who had 'no money but a lot of time on his hands'. I guess he had lost his job. He had been walking through the area since January, sleeping at night wherever he found a cave. Tomorrow, thirty kilometres downstream, I will visit the Chauvet cave which was rediscovered for the first time since the last ice age in 1994. And there I will be looking at the oldest known rock paintings in the world, 15,000 years older than the paintings of Lascaux or Altamira.

During a relatively warm period in the last ice age the climate here was between 3° C and 5° C colder than it is today. The trees were limited to birches, Scots pine and juniper. The fauna included many species who are now extinct: mammoths, megaceros deer, cave lions without manes, aurochs and bears who were three metres tall, as well as reindeer, ibex, bison, rhinoceros and wild horses. The human population of nomadic hunter-gatherers was sparse and lived in groups of about twenty to twenty-five. Paleontologists name this population Cro-Magnon, a term which distances, yet the distance between them and us may be less than we think. Neither agriculture nor metallurgy existed. Music and jewellery did. The average life expectancy was twenty-five.

The need for companionship while alive was the same.

The Cro-Magnon reply, however, to the first and perennial human question of: Where are we? was different from ours. The nomads were acutely aware of being a minority who were overwhelmingly outnumbered by animals. They had been born, not on to a planet, but *into* animal life. They were not animal keepers: animals were the keepers of the world and of the universe around them which never stopped. Beyond every horizon were more animals.

At the same time, they were distinct from animals. They could make fire and therefore had light in the darkness. They could kill at a distance. They fashioned many things with their hands. They made tents for themselves, held up by mammoth bones. They spoke. They could count. They could carry water. They died differently. Their exemption from animals was possible because they were a minority, and, as such, the animals could pardon them for this exemption.

At the beginning of the Ardèche gorges is the Pont d'Arc, a bridge whose almost symmetrical 34-metre-high arch has been carved out by the river itself. On the southern bank stands a tall outcrop of limestone whose weathered silhouette suggests a giant in a cloak striding towards the bridge in order to cross it. Behind him on the rock face are yellow and red stains – ochre and iron oxide – painted by the rain. If the giant were to cross the bridge, he would almost immediately, given his size, find himself up against the opposite cliffs, near the top of which he would find the Chauvet cave.

Both bridge and giant were there at the time of the Cro-Magnons. The only difference being that 30,000 years ago, when the paintings were being painted, the Ardèche meandered up to the foot of the cliffs, and the natural path which I am climbing would regularly have been crossed by animals coming down, species by species, to drink from the river. The cave was strategically and magically placed.

The Cro-Magnons lived with fear and amazement in a culture of Arrival, facing many mysteries. Their culture lasted for some 20,000 years. We live in a culture of ceaseless Departure and Progress which has so far lasted two or three centuries. Today's culture, instead of facing mysteries, persistently tries to outflank them.

Silence. I turn off the helmet lamp. A darkness. In the darkness the silence becomes encyclopedic, condensing everything that has occurred in the interval between then and now.

On a rock in front of me, a cluster of red squarish dots. The freshness of the red is startling. As present and immediate as a smell, or as the colour of flowers on a June evening when the sun is going down. These dots were made by applying red oxide pigment to the palm of a hand and then pressing it against the rock. One particular hand has been identified on account of a disjointed little finger, and another imprint of the same hand has been found elsewhere in the cave.

On another rock, similar dots, making an overall shape which is like the side view of a bison. The marks of the hands fill the animal's body.

Darkness.

Before the women, men and children arrived (there is a footprint of a child of about eleven in the cave) and after they left for good, the place was inhabited by bears. Probably also by wolves and other animals, but the bears were the masters with whom the nomads had to share the cave. On wall after wall, the scratches of bear paws. Footprints show where a bear walked with her cub, feeling her way in the dark. In the largest and most central of the cave's chambers, which is fifteen metres high, there are numerous wallows or depressions in the clay on the ground where bears lay asleep during their winter hibernation. One hundred and fifty bear skulls have been found here. One of them had been solemnly placed – probably by a Cro-Magnon – on a kind of rock plinth in the furthest reach of the cave.

Silence.

In the silence, the extent and size of the place begins to count for more and more. The cave is half a kilometre long and sometimes fifty metres wide. Geometrical measurements, however, do not apply because one is inside something like a body.

The standing and overhanging rocks, the enclosing walls, with their concretions, the passages, the hollow spaces which have developed through the geological process of diagenesis, resemble, to a remarkable degree, the organs and spaces within a human or animal body. What they all have in common is that they look like forms created by flowing water.

The colours of the cave too are anatomical. The carbonate rocks are bone- and tripe-coloured, the stalagmites scarlet and very white, the calcite draperies and concretions orange and snotty. Surfaces glisten as if wet with mucus.

A massive stalactite has grown (they grow at the rate of one centimetre per century) to look somewhat like a stomach's intestines, and, at one point in their descent, the tubes suggest the four legs, tail and trunk of a miniature mammoth. The reference could easily be missed and so a Cro-Magnon painter, with four brief lines in red, brought the tiny mammoth nearer.

Many walls that might have lent themselves to being painted on have not been touched. The 400-odd animals depicted here are distributed as unobtrusively as in nature. There are no pictorial displays as in Lascaux or Altamira. There is more emptiness, more secrecy, perhaps greater complicity with the darkness. Yet, although these paintings are 15,000 years earlier, they are, mostly, as skilful, observant and graceful as any of the later paintings. Art, it would seem, is born like a foal who can walk straight away. The talent to make art accompanies the need for that art; they arrive together.

I crawl into a low cup-shaped annex – four metres in diameter – and there, drawn in red on its irregular curving sides, are three bears – male, female and cub, as in the fairy story to be told many millennia later. I squat there, watching. Three bears and behind them two small ibex. The artist conversed with the rock by the flickering light of his charcoal torch. A protruding bulge allowed the bear's forepaw to swing outwards with its awesome weight as it lolloped forward. A fissure followed precisely the line of an ibex's back. The artist knew these animals absolutely and intimately; his *hands* could visualise them in the dark. What the rock told him was that the animals – like everything else which existed – were inside the rock, and that he, with his red pigment on his finger, could persuade them to come to the rock's surface, to its membrane surface, to brush against it and stain it with their smells.

Today, due to the humidity of the atmosphere, many of the painted surfaces have become as sensitive as a membrane, and could easily be wiped off with a rag. Hence the reverence.

Step outside the cave and re-enter the wind rush of time passing. Re-assume names. Inside the cave everything is present and nameless. Inside the cave there is fear, but the fear is in perfect balance with a sense of protection.

The Cro-Magnons did not live in the cave. They entered it to participate in certain rites, about which little is known. The suggestion that they were, in some way, shamanistic seems convincing. The number of people in the cave at any given time may never have exceeded thirty.

How frequently did they come? Did generations of artists work here? No answers. Perhaps we have to be content with intuiting that they came here to experience, and to carry away with them in memory, special moments of living a perfect balance between danger and survival, fear and a sense of protection? Can one hope for more at any time?

Most of the animals depicted in Chauvet were in life ferocious, yet nowhere in their depiction is there a trace of fear. Respect, yes, a fraternal, intimate respect. And this is why in every animal image here there is a human presence. A presence revealed by pleasure. Each creature here is at home in man – a strange formulation, yet incontestable.

In the furthest chamber – two lions drawn with charcoal in black. Approximately life size. They stand side by side in profile, the male behind, and the female, touching the length of him and parallel to him, nearer to me.

They are here as a single, incomplete (their forelegs and back paws are missing and, I suspect, were never drawn) yet total presence. The rock face around them, which is naturally lion-coloured, has become lion.

I try to draw the two of them. The lioness is both beside the lion, rubbing herself against him, and inside him. And this ambivalence is the result of the most cunning elision, whereby the two animals share a contour. The low contour of loin, belly and chest belongs to them both – and they share it with an animal grace.

For the rest, their contours are separate. The lines of their tails, backs, necks, foreheads, muzzles are independent, approaching one another, parting, converging and ending at different points, for the lion is much longer than the lioness.

Two standing animals, male and female, joined below by the single line of their bellies, where they are most vulnerable and have less fur.

I'm drawing on absorbent Japanese paper which I chose because I thought the difficulty of drawing with black ink on such paper might take me a little closer to the difficulties of drawing with charcoal (which was burnt and made here in the cave) on rough rock surfaces. In both cases the line is never quite obedient. One has to nudge, cajole.

Two reindeer are stepping in opposite directions – east and west. They do not share a contour, instead they are drawn over each other, so that the upper one's forelegs cross like large ribs the flank of the lower one. And they are inseparable, their two bodies are locked into the same hexagon, the little tail of the upper one rhyming with the antlers of lower one, the long head, with a profile like a flint burin, of the upper one whistling to the metatarsus of the other's hind leg. They are making a single sign, and they are dancing in a circle.

When the drawing was almost complete, the artist abandoned charcoal and painted and rubbed in with his finger a thick black (the colour of your hair after swimming) along the lower one's belly and dewlap. Then he did the same thing with the upper animal, mixing the paint with the whitish sediment on the rock so that it was less violent.

As I draw, I ask myself whether my hand, obeying the

visible rhythm of the reindeer's dance, may not be dancing with the hand that first drew them?

It is still possible here to come upon a crumb of broken charcoal which fell to the floor when a line was being drawn.

What makes Chauvet unique is the fact that it was sealed off. The roof of the original entrance chamber – which was spacious and penetrated by daylight – collapsed some 20,000 years ago. And from then until 1994 the darkness which the artists had addressed, because it was at the far edge of their reach, entered from *behind* to bury and preserve everything they had made.

The stalagmites and stalactites continued to grow. In places films of calcite covered, like cataracts, some details. For the most part, however, the extraordinary freshness of what was traced remains. And this immediacy sabotages any linear sense of time.

I come upon a small overhanging rock which is shaped like the tip of a pancreas and on it are two red paintings, probably of butterflies.

Anne, who is dying in Cambridge, comes to my mind. Her husband, Simon's father, was a professor of archeology. A long while ago she used to camp, summer after summer, beside Palaeolithic sites.

So, if the dates are right, the paintings you're looking at are from the same time as the sculpted woman of Willendorf?

Yes.

Sculpted from reddish limestone if my memory isn't playing me tricks.

It isn't playing tricks.

The morphine makes you fuzzy. Have they found many flint axes?

I'm not sure. Maybe a dozen.

Making a flint axe symmetrical was already the beginning of art.

I'm trying to say that.

I want Anne at this moment, this very moment, to see from her bed the red butterfly.

Several herds heading west. Among them, near animals, drawn very small, touch gigantic faraway animals.

In the dry season a well-laid fire, once lit, can catch so quickly that those watching it can feel the air being swept away.

Cro-Magnon painting did not respect borders. It flows where it has to, deposits, overlaps, submerges images already there, and it continually changes the scale of what it carries. What kind of imaginative space did the Cro-Magnons live in?

For nomads the notion of past and future is subservient to the experience of *elsewhere*. Something that has gone, or is awaited, is hidden elsewhere in another place.

For both hunters and hunted hiding well is the precondition for survival. Life depends upon finding cover. Everything hides. What has vanished has gone into hiding. An absence – as after the departure of the dead – is felt as a loss but not as an abandonment. The dead are hiding elsewhere.

A male ibex, with curved horns as long as its body, has been drawn with charcoal on whitish rock. How to describe the blackness of its traces? It is a blackness which makes the darkness reassuring, a blackness which is a lining for the immemorial. He is walking up a gentle incline, his steps delicate, his body rounded, his face flat. Each line is as tense as a well thrown rope, and the drawing has a double energy which is perfectly shared: the energy of the animal who has become present, and that of the man whose arm and eye are drawing the animal by torch light.

These rock paintings were made where they were, so that they might exist in the dark. They were *for* the dark.

They were hidden in the dark so that what they embodied would outlast everything visible, and promise, perhaps, survival.

What they painted is like a map, Anne says.
   Of what?
   The company in the dark.
   Who are where?
   Here, come from elsewhere . . .

7

Madrid

I am waiting for my friend Juan who will, I think, be late.
His statues are never late; they are always already there,
enigmatically waiting at the rendezvous. Juan works like
a mechanic in a small garage, lying on his back as if
underneath a car; he looks at his watch only when he
crawls out and gets to his feet. We have agreed to meet in
the lounge of the Ritz Hotel, Madrid.

There are tall palms and, leading off this lounge, a bar
named after Velásquez. (I doubt whether he drank
much.) The walls, the columns, the conservatory ceiling,
are painted a whitish-yellow, not what the paint manu-
facturers call *ivory*, but the true colour of elephant's tusks
– much closer to the colour of old teeth. The ceiling of the
lounge is as high as three elephants standing on each
other's backs.

As soon as one comes off the street and the double glass
doors swing shut, one is aware here of the deafness of
money, which, like the depth of an ocean, is perceived not
as an empty silence, but as a seclusion.

The wide, carpeted staircase and, upstairs, the suites

and bedrooms with their shaving mirrors which enlarge many times and yet nevertheless flatter – an optical laboratory must have worked for months to meet that challenge – are palpably quiet. In the lounge, although a number of people are talking, their voices are muted, just as the hands of the two waiters, carrying tinkling trays of glasses full of champagne, are gloved. They wear white gloves.

The first guests for an evening reception are arriving. The reception is being held to launch the new Venezuelan economy, which, supposedly, now depends on Spanish investors.

The seclusion prompts me to remember the Cma of shanty towns and the everlasting racket in prisons.

The reception guests, mostly in their thirties, have surf-riding smiles, controlled eyes and a way of tilting themselves forward like the figureheads once carved on ships. In the muted quiet, cameramen and journalists, with their microphones at the ready, are waiting for the stars who have promised to attend.

Not far from where I'm sitting, three hotel guests, who apparently have nothing to do with the reception, have installed themselves on two sofas and a deep armchair, as if they were at home. Perhaps they never leave their home but carry it with them like snails: snails who have lived a long while and have ancient names.

Both waiters and cameramen are respecting their claimed territory. On the floor between the two sofas is a large Chinese carpet, and the man of the trio, who is also the youngest, paces slowly round this Chinese carpet, smoking a Cuban cigar.

Those invited to launch the new economy are all, women and men, agents of promotion, and perhaps it is the imaginative effort of promotion that obliges them to lean forward in the way they do.

It may happen, at the end of a long day, that one of them catches a glimpse of himself reflected in a glass, and that then this leaning forward provokes a kind of paralysing panic – a fear of falling forwards, flat on one's face! (A similar panic is sometimes visible on the faces of those suffering from Parkinson's.) This evening, however, they are confident as they lean forward to take the glasses of champagne from the tray offered them by the waiters with white gloves.

For the man with the Cuban cigar, smoking is a way of slowing down the process – or at least his awareness of the process – of things getting steadily worse.

A young woman, seated on an upright chair opposite me, is reading a book. Like me, she is waiting for somebody who is late, though she looks towards the door more frequently than I do. I suspect she is waiting for somebody she's in love with, and whom she doubts will turn up this evening. The crescendo of her disappointment is expressed by the ever briefer glances she accords to the book. Suddenly she slaps it shut, gets to her feet, and walks out between the camera-lights, set up for the stars.

I see him coming down the wide staircase, a room key

dangling from his lightly clenched fist. The way he holds the key, it could be a bird he has in his hand. He is wearing a checked cap, tweed jacket, plus fours with heavy woollen socks and brogue shoes. His name is Tyler. His first name escapes me – probably because I remember that it signified a lot. His first name – whatever it was – evoked the mystery that surrounded him, above all, the mystery of the defeat he had suffered. I always addressed him as Sir.

Tyler is now at the bottom of the staircase and has taken off his cap and is coming into the lounge. As I follow him with my eyes, he looks away. He had a great gift for looking away and avoiding questions. He chooses the chair vacated by the woman who decided she would wait no longer for her lover. There he picks up a menu for drinks and sandwiches and studies it through his thick glasses, bringing it close up to his forehead. Often when he dropped some small object – the stub of a pencil, or a rubber – it was I who would look for it on the floor, because he could not see without bending down. Once the frame of his glasses broke – it was a very cold winter – and I mended them for him with some sticking plaster which we bought at a chemist shop. This was in 1932 or 1933. I was six years old. Now he turns the chair he has chosen so that he is not facing me, and gives his order to a waiter.

On one of the trio's sofas, with skeletal legs crossed, and a shoe dangling from an arched foot, reclines a woman of over eighty with platinum hair. She might be the cigar-smoker's mother. She too is smoking – her cigarette in a long holder – to slow down the process of things getting steadily worse. Being, however, older than he – and possibly his mother – she is more confident that she herself won't live to see the worst.

The skin of her face and neck, after numerous operations, is like crêpe de Chine paper. Her head – chin up as she exhales the cigarette smoke – reposes on a cushion. Her left arm is draped along the long back of the sofa and the flesh of her arm is draped from its three bones. She is wearing half a dozen golden bracelets and a pearl necklace.

Hard to know whether the pearls are real, as hard as it is to guess whether she comes from a circus or a château. Both would allow her her special effrontery, which is full of disdain and pride in all the appetites she has not lost and is determined to satisfy.

Maybe Circe on her island of Aeaea was more like this than the way she is usually depicted, centuries later, in Renaissance paintings.

The third member of the trio is the confidante, at least for this evening and, who knows? perhaps for life, of Circe. Maybe she is her sister, Pasiphae, the one who had an affair with the Bull of Crete and gave birth to the Minotaur. It is impossible to guess the age of this person, tumbled into the massive armchair beside the sofa, because of her size. Her immensity seems like that of time itself. She wears rings on seven fingers. Her neck is as wide as a slender woman's waist. From time to time she glances protectively at Circe. In her expression there is less disdain than in her sister's, since other people impinge on her less. She notices only those who approach close to her, and so she is spared the gaping curiosity which must be her lot as soon as she appears anywhere in public.

She has learnt to answer the question that used to haunt her: Where am I? She now knows the answer by heart: I'm here, I am here in the centre of myself. And this is her effrontery.

The waiter brings Tyler a bottle of white wine in an ice bucket and a silver stand of sandwiches decorated with parsley.

An actress, accompanied by three men, and wearing a backless dress, makes her entrance into the lounge. She is resplendently pregnant. In answer to a journalist's question, she gently pokes a finger to make a dimple in her belly, and says: The middle of June! The public applaud.

A waiter asks me whether I would like to order something. I do so. After a moment I hear Tyler's voice: I regret to see that you have not improved your pronunciation. You are as lost in Spanish as you once were in English, he says.

I do my best, Sir.

You don't listen to how other people talk. You never say to yourself: He speaks well, so I'll listen to him and learn how to speak.

I listen all the time, Sir.

You don't listen with enough patience.

I can listen for hours.

Then why do you pronounce so badly?

I don't listen to their words, Sir.

Exactly.

During this conversation Tyler sips his wine and doesn't glance in my direction for a second. Circe is eyeing him with some interest. She is probably telling herself that he is only half her age, and that he is so evidently a gentleman he will ignore the difference.

If you want to catch a ball, Tyler explained to us in the Green Hut, you don't snatch at it in the air, you watch it coming and then place your hands accordingly. The Hut was roofed with corrugated iron which was painted green. It had a door that fitted badly and three small windows. There was no heating and no water. Tyler and I brought the water each day in his car. What did we do about shitting? I don't remember. Maybe there was an earth closet outside. A vague memory of vomiting there once. This hut on the edge of a field was our school. Nobody, however, referred to it as such, because Tyler insisted that he was not a schoolmaster but a tutor. A tutor in a green hut.

A young government minister has arrived. He is surveying the lounge to see who else is there. In a minute he will decide whether to make his entrance straight away, or whether to wait for a moment in the Velásquez bar. His bodyguards too are surveying everyone in the lounge and in the entrance hall and at the hotel reception desk. For them to recognise a face, or place somebody, is already a distraction, for the shot, the blow, may come from anybody or anywhere in the world.

It was in the Green Hut before the eyes of Tyler, now eating his sandwiches decorated with parsley in the lounge of the Ritz Hotel, Madrid, that I first learnt to write. Earlier, at a nursery school, I had learnt to form the letters, all of them, from A to Z, belonging like moles or birthmarks or beauty spots to the pert, pretty, rounded body of my teacher, Lilles, whom I loved. Forming the letters, however, was not writing, as Tyler pointed out on my first day in the Green Hut. Writing involves spelling, straight lines, spacing, words leaning the right way, margins, size, legibility, keeping the nib clean, never making blots, and demonstrating on each page of the exercise book the value of good manners.

We were six boys, all from different families. Wood. Henry. Blagdon. Bowes-Lyon. And one I've forgotten. For every lesson we sat at the same small table. Tyler, when he wasn't looking over our shoulders, stood behind the workbench on which, twice a week, we learnt carpentry.

Most educational establishments are mysterious, perhaps because teaching and folly share an interface. And the Green Hut was no exception. I still don't know how the place began, how long it had existed before I was sent there, where Tyler came from. He coached boys to get into what were considered good schools. I don't think my parents – unlike the others – paid any fees. I think he ate free in my mother's café in exchange for his improving my English and making it possible to pass me off as a gentleman boy. We both recognised the hopelessness of the project – I was with him for two and a half years – and this was our secret, which made us, in a strange way, accomplices.

You're going to make a mess of your life.

Why, Sir?

Because you can't saw straight.

It's difficult to hold, Sir.

Only because you're scared of its teeth. Are you frightened of sawing your thumb off?

No, Sir.

Then saw straight.

Apart from carpentry, we learnt arithmetic, geometry, Latin, drawing, the history of the Royal Family, geography, physics and gardening.

How do you spell hyacinth?

With a 'y', Sir.

Of course. But where is the 'y'? You're in too much of a hurry. Let the question sink in. Take the measure of it.

During the winter in the Green Hut, the six of us suffered from the cold. There was only a portable paraffin stove, nothing more. And on certain days the can of paraffin was empty. Tyler would pretend he had forgotten, because he preferred us to think that he was absentminded rather than broke. We had red noses, chilblains on our fingers and toes, and sopping handkerchiefs stuffed into the pockets of our shorts. In the months of January and February Tyler often wore a long loosely knitted woollen scarf whose colours astounded us: white and lilac with little flecks of pink – the colours you see mixed with snot on your handkerchief after your nose has stopped bleeding.

After the last lesson of the afternoon in the Hut, driving in his car to his home, from where later I caught the bus to mine, he would offer me, as I sat beside him, half of this scarf.

Where did it come from, Sir?

You ask too many questions. You do it to draw attention to yourself.

I'm interested, Sir.

You never stop being interested, that's where the trouble begins. Wrap this end around you, keep quiet, and put your gloves on.

Circe sits up, and, with a flick of her head, tosses her hair back.

Señor, she asks Tyler, do you find the sandwiches here good?

The bread is a little too thinly cut, but otherwise, yes, Señora.

She gazes at him shamelessly; the elegance and sadness of his reply allow it.

Tyler's car was an Austin 7. The roof was a kind of tarpaulin, with brackets that folded. On winter mornings he had to start it by turning the crank handle. I sat in the driver's seat, on the very edge, so that my right foot could touch the accelerator if the engine caught. Sometimes it took us ten minutes. I would shiver, and his moustache got frosted.

Tyler lived in two rented rooms on the ground floor of

a large house with a rose garden he did not have the right to sit in. The house belonged to a widow whom I occasionally glimpsed wearing a fur coat or a floral summer dress. She, like Tyler, was a Catholic, which is why she agreed to rent him the two small rooms. He was allowed to leave his car in the drive, but only in one place, at the back of the house by the kitchen door where the dustbins were.

We'll be leaving tomorrow, Circe says, touching the shoulder of Tyler's tweed jacket, leaving for Huesca. I feel, Señor, that you would love Aragon. You might accompany us?

The cigar smoker – Telegonus if he's really the blonde's son – is now helping to get Pasiphae out of her chair and on to her feet. It is a struggle, and they need both of her crutches, which fit under her elbows, to prop her upright. Once on her feet, she turns towards Tyler.

I think you would enjoy seeing our horses, she says.

Once more I wonder whether they come from a circus or a château.

Tyler's two rented rooms smelt, like the Green Hut, of his cigarettes. He smoked a brand called De Resque Minor. On the windowsills of the two rooms he grew flowers in wooden boxes. On the mantelpiece, there were often plant-cuttings in tumblers, each with a little label attached to it, with its name written in his meticulous rounded handwriting: Red Campion. Sweet Sultan. Phlox. Larkspur.

It would have given him pleasure if I had been able to

remember the Latin name of just one of them, but there, in his living quarters, lessons were out of the question. So larkspur remained larkspur. In the Green Hut Tyler demanded work and obedience; the smallest sign of what he called *slackness* would be punished by a rap over the knuckles with a knotted yew branch that hung on a hook beside the cupboard where he kept the rulers and exercise books. In his two living rooms slackness was ignored and he demanded only quiet and company.

He spread honey – given to him by a beekeeping friend – on to a slice of toast, toasted in front of the gas fire, and he offered it to me on a hand-painted plate.

The plate was decorated by a friend of mine, he said. You recognise the plant?

Not yet, Sir.

The flower of the so-called Strawberry Tree.

Strawberries on a tree, Sir?

He didn't bother to reply.

Tyler made drawings himself. Always with an HB pencil. Sketches of Tudor cottages, churches, driveways, willow trees, sheep, delphiniums. Some of his drawings he had printed on postcards.

Do you sell them, Sir?

I print them for my friends, like this I can offer them a little present.

Nobody can help him, I told myself, as I sat in the wicker chair before his gas fire, rubbing my chilblains and eating my toast and honey. He's too old and he has too many hairs growing out of his body.

Pasiphae on her two sticks is crossing the reception. People make way for her, and, when she stops to regain her breath, they move around her as if she were a natural landmark. It is her effrontery which puts them at ease.

Did she die?

Who are you talking about? Tyler asked.

I nodded towards a photograph by his bed.

Never, never, talk, he said, about what you see on somebody's bedside table. Study it if you want to – he picked up the framed photograph and put it in my hands – remember it if you like, but say nothing, for there's nothing to be said. Nothing.

At last the TV star arrives. People have been standing in the street outside the hotel for almost an hour in the hope of catching a glimpse of her. She is tiny, even smaller than they thought, perfect, with tumbling black hair, wearing silver. Cameras flash on all sides. We all of us hope to find – in this impromptu unscreened moment – something beyond the fame, something which equalises. For example: the fact that she too farts like us. Meanwhile, we are also waiting for the opposite to happen: she has so much perfection, much more than any single person needs, so she could throw some to us!

Tyler takes a pad out of his pocket and begins to draw one of the palm trees in the hotel lounge.

It is at this moment, as he begins to draw, that I remember the weight of his solitude. Perhaps with me, given my age, he felt no need to mask or hide it. Anyway, his glasses magnified the solitude expressed in his eyes.

The man who taught me to write was the first person to make me aware of irreparable loss.

Pasiphae is returning on her crutches from the Velásquez bar. Did she have a drink there? When she reaches her chair, she has the problem of lowering herself. Telegonus is at the ready, but it is safer to have a man on each side, so she glances at Tyler, who immediately comes and places one of his huge hands under her colossal elbow.

Are you an artist, Señor?

No, it's a pastime, Señora.

The TV star, accompanied by a guitarist, has started to sing. The tune is both very young and very old. She sings simply, her eyes almost shut, her silver hips almost still, her lips almost touching the microphone.

> On a tree trunk
> a young girl jubilant
> carved her name . . .
> you are she who cut into my bark . . .

Tyler died in his fifties soon after the Second World War.

His death involved a story about a gas fire, or a house burning down, or an accident with a car left running in a garage with the doors shut. I have forgotten the details because they suggested that the methodical, tidy, gruffly shy man, who believed that quality mattered more than anything else in the world, died – or even put an end to his days – through indifference or carelessness. The details are better forgotten.

We'll be leaving shortly, Circe whispers, standing at his elbow. It's a big car and there's plenty of room for your luggage.

I have very little, Señora.

So you will come and draw our horses? Pasiphae asks him.

When you shade a drawing, you do not scribble. Is that clear? You shade carefully, putting one line beside the next and the next and the next. Then you crosshatch and that way your lines weave the sketch together. The verb: to weave. Past participle?

Woven, Sir.

Juan comes up behind me, puts his hands over my eyes and demands: Who is it?

8

The Szum and the Ching

We've arrived – if you are with me. We're going no
further. We've reached the house with no doorstep in
what they call Little Poland.

I often thought the road-signs were telling a fairy tale:
Double Bend, Leaping Deer, Cross Roads, Level Cross-
ing, Roundabout, Falling Stones, Steep Hill, Wandering
Cattle, Dangerous Corner.

The warnings offered, when compared to the risks of
life, seemed to be of a reassuring simplicity.

It's hard to say what changes in the sky when driving
eastwards after Berlin. You begin to notice whatever is
vertical against the flatness of the plain in a different way:
the wooden fences, a man standing in a field, the occasional horse, the trees in a forest. The distance you see in
the sky is no longer saying the same things as before; here
it is announcing that, after another few thousand kilometres, the plain is going to become the steppe – and on

the steppe distance becomes as dangerous and challenging as altitude in the mountains.

On the steppe trees grow tougher and smaller, just as certain trees do on mountains – the Carpathians to the south for instance – so as to resist the winter. There are birches on the steppe no taller than a dog. On the mountains the ferocious cold is due to the altitude; on the steppe it is due to the distances, the horizontal extent of the continent.

After crossing the Oder this extent, this extension, is promised, even if not yet there. The sky is making a new proposition to the earth.

I am heading eastwards on my bike along the main road, which joins Warsaw and Moscow. The traffic in both directions is heavy. In a few years' time this will be a motorway. The road skirts or crosses many forests. Northern ones, in which the summer light is green and the trunks of the spruces as they grow taller become more and more a feathery orange colour. What coral is to fishes, the tops of these red spruces may be to birds.

The number of lives that enter our own is incalculable.

Young women are standing on the shoulder of the road, dressed to kill, hips thrust to the side, beckoning to the drivers coming westwards. A man driving an old, battered 123 Mercedes has stopped. The Poles call this car a *beczka*, which means a barrel. The driver, who is Ukrainian, also looks like a barrel. Most of the girls are Romanian. The services are paid for in dollar bills.

OK, she says, holding out her hand for the money.

Afterwards, he says, refusing to pay now. What's your name?

In her backless dress, she shrugs her shoulders.

He points to himself, stubbing his chest with his thumb. Mickhail, he says, I'm called Mickhail. You?

She shakes her head and examines her face in the driving mirror.

Your name?

She replies with the English phrase, used in all situations when she reckons it's best to withdraw. I dunno, she says.

Fed up, he opens the door of the car and she has to get out. Whereupon he drives off fast, making the tyres slip and throw up dust.

Another young woman walks out from behind the trees. She is holding the hand of an elderly man who is wearing a felt hat with a feather in it. The two girls work this little stretch of forest together.

Hi! Lenuta! the one with the old man calls out to the one who had no luck with the Ukrainian. Do you know what the bastards have done?

What?

They have pinched his car. I take him into the forest. I bring him back and it's gone. A new BMW 525.

Is he blaming you?

He's German and I fear he may have a heart attack.

He's paid you? Lenuta asks.

The other one nods.

Then leave him!

The other one pulls a face and shrugs her shoulders.

So give him to me, says Lenuta, and go and see Janey – maybe Evgen knows something about the car.

The man sits down on the ferns. He stares at his boots and puts a hand on his chest. Lenuta takes off his hat with the feather in it and, holding it by the brim, fans him. It's 40° C.

An old woman accompanied by a small boy emerges from the forest. Her fingers and thumbs are stained purple. The boy is carrying a supermarket carrier-bag. They have been picking blueberries. And in a moment the boy will sit on the roadside with four one-litre jars, filled with the black fruit they have gathered.

I have a friend who is an ethologist. Not long ago she worked for years with the wolves in the Białowieza forest, about 200 kilometres east from here. Over many months, patiently and fearlessly, she sidled up to the wolves until they accepted her, until their curiosity became keener than their wariness. Her name is Despina. Early one morning the pack-leader, whom she called Siber, approached and showed her he wanted her to follow him. She complied. He led her slowly, glancing back over his shoulder to make sure she was following, through the undergrowth of the forest, to the lair in the earth, where his she-wolf had given birth to their cubs. By now they were two weeks old, and on the morning in question the mother was about to bring them out of the lair to introduce them for the first time to the rest of the pack, three other wolves who were there in front of Despina, waiting for the encounter. Siber and his mate called the cubs out. Yuuuer . . . yuuer . . . yuue. One by one they emerged, eyes searching. After they are three weeks old cubs become suspicious of any creature who is not recognisable as a member of the pack, so this was the moment for them to meet. And Siber wanted Despina to witness that moment.

Not too close to the girls, the grandmother warns her grandson with his jar of blueberries. Keep away from the Romanian girls, otherwise when there are women in the cars they won't let their men stop.

Everybody in this land sells or tries to sell something. Men in their sixties stand on the kerb in the large towns towards evening, holding up a piece of cardboard on which they've written the word: *POKOJE*. They are trying to sell the guest room in their small flat or house for one night to a passing traveller.

Each jar of berries costs eight złoty.

The BMW has been recovered. The elderly German forks out several hundred złoty. He's wearing his hat with the feather in it again and is minutely examining his car's tyres – probably to make sure that they have not been changed.

The roads are straight, the distance between towns long. The sky is making a new proposition to the earth. I imagine travelling alone between Kalisz and Kielce a hundred and fifty years ago. Between the two names there would always have been a third – the name of your horse. Your horse's name the constant between the names of the towns you approach and the towns you leave behind.

I see a sign for Tarnów to the south. At the end of the nineteenth century Abraham Bredius, the compiler of the first modern catalogue of Rembrandt paintings, discovered a canvas in a castle there.

'When I saw a magnificent four-in-hand passing my hotel and learnt from the porter that it was Count Tarnowski who had become engaged some days before to the ravishing Countess Potocka, who would bring him a considerable dowry, I had little idea that this man was also the fortunate owner of one of the most sublime works by our great master.'

Bredius left the hotel and made a long and difficult

journey by train – he complained that for miles the train travelled at a walking pace – to the Count's castle. There he spotted a canvas of a horse and rider, which he unhesitatingly attributed to Rembrandt, considering it a masterpiece that had been forgotten for a century. It was given the title of *The Polish Rider*.

Nobody today knows precisely who or what the painting represented for the painter. The rider's coat is typically Polish – a *kontusz*. Likewise the rider's headgear. This is probably why the painting was bought by a Polish nobleman in Amsterdam, and taken to Poland at the end of the eighteenth century.

When I first saw the painting in the Frick Collection in New York, where it ended up, I felt it might be a portrait of Rembrandt's beloved son, Titus. It seemed to me – and it still does – a painting about leaving home.

A more scholarly theory suggests that the painting may have been inspired by a Pole, Jonaz Szlichtyng, who, during Rembrandt's time in Amsterdam, was something of a rebel-hero in dissident circles. Szlichtyng belonged to a sect that followed the sixteenth-century Sienese theologian Lebo Sozznisi, who denied that Christ was the son of God – for, if he were, the religion would cease to be monotheistic. If the painting was inspired by Jonaz Szlichtyng it offers an image of a Christlike figure, who is a man, only a man, setting out, mounted on a horse, to meet his destiny.

Do you think you are going fast enough to get away from me? she asks as she draws up beside me at the first traffic light in Kielce.

I notice that she is driving with her shoes kicked off, her bare feet on the pedals.

No question of leaving you behind, I say, straightening my back and putting both feet on the ground.

Then why so fast?

I don't reply, for she knows the answer.

In speed there is a forgotten tenderness. She had a way, when driving, of lifting her right hand from the steering wheel so that she could see the dials on the dashboard without having to move her head a centimetre. And this small movement of her hand was as neat and precise as that of a great conductor before an orchestra. I loved her surety.

When she was alive I called her Liz, and she called me Met. She liked the nickname Liz because during her life up to that moment it would have been inconceivable that she should answer to such a vulgar abbreviation. 'Liz' implied a law had been broken and she adored broken laws.

Met is the name given to a flight navigator in a novel by Saint-Exupéry. Perhaps *Vol de Nuit*. She was much better read than I, but I was more street-wise, and perhaps this is why she named me after a navigator. The idea of calling me Met came to her while driving through Calabria. Whenever we got out of the car she put on a hat with a wide brim. She detested suntan. Her skin was as pale as the Spanish royal family's in the time of Velásquez.

What brought us together? Superficially it was curiosity – almost everything about us, including our ages, was undisguisedly different. Between us there were many first times. Yet more profoundly, it was an unspoken acknowledgement of the same sadness which brought us together. There was no self-pity. If she had perceived a trace of this in me she would have cauterised it. And I, as I say, loved her surety, which is incompatible with self-pity. A sadness that was like the crazy howl of a dog at the full moon.

For different reasons, the two of us believed that style was indispensable for living with a little hope, and either you lived with hope or in despair. There was no middle way.

Style? A certain lightness. A sense of shame excluding certain actions or reactions. A certain proposition of elegance. The supposition that, despite everything, a melody can be looked for and sometimes found. Style is tenuous, however. It comes from within. You can't go out and acquire it. Style and fashion may share a dream, but they are created differently. Style is about an invisible promise. This is why it requires and encourages a talent for endurance and an ease with time. Style is very close to music.

We spent evenings listening wordlessly to Bartók, Walton, Britten, Shostakovich, Chopin, Beethoven.

Hundreds of evenings. It was the period of 33″ records which one had to turn over by hand. And those moments of turning the record over, and slowly lowering the arm with its diamond needle, were moments of a hallucinating plenitude, grateful and expectant, only comparable with the other moments, also wordless, when one of us was on top of the other making love.

So, why the howl? Style comes from within, yet style has to borrow its assurance from another time and then lend it to the present, and the borrower has to leave a pledge with that other time. The passionate present is invariably too short for style. Liz, aristocrat that she was, borrowed from the past, and I borrowed from a revolutionary future.

Our two styles were surprisingly close. I'm not thinking about the accoutrements of life or brand names. I'm remembering how we were when walking through a forest drenched by rain, or when arriving at Milan's central railway station in the small hours of the morning. Very close.

Yet when we looked deeply into one another's eyes, defying the risks involved in this, of which we were fully aware, both of us came to realise that the times being borrowed from were chimera. This was the sadness. This is what made the dog howl.

The traffic light turns green. I overtake her and she follows. After we've left Kielce behind, I give a sign to announce I'm going to stop. We both pull up along the edge of another forest, darker than the last one. Her car window is already down. The very fine hair by her temple, sweeping back behind her ear, is delicately tangled. Delicately because to untangle it with my fingers would require delicacy. Around the glove compartment of the dashboard she has stuck different coloured feathers.

Met, she says, there were days on end, you remember, when we got rid of the vulgarity of History. Then after a while, you'd go back, deserting me, again and again. You were addicted.

To what?

You were addicted – she touches several of the feathers with her fingers – you were addicted to the making of history, and you chose to ignore that those who believe they're making history already have their hands on power, or imagine having their hands on power, and that this power, as sure as the night is long, Met, will confuse them! After a year or so they won't know what they're doing. She lets her hand fall on to her thigh.

History has to be endured, she goes on, has to be endured with pride, an absurd pride that is also – God knows why – invincible. In Europe the Poles are the centuries-old specialists in such an endurance. That is why I love them. I've loved them since I met pilots from Squadron 303 during the war. I never questioned them, I listened to them. And when they asked me, I danced with them.

A wooden dray loaded down with new timber emerges from the forest. The pair of horses are covered with lather and sweat because the wheels sink deep into the soft earth of the forest track.

The soul of this place has a lot to do with horses, she says, laughing. And you with your famous historical laws, you didn't know any better than Trotsky how to rub down a horse! Maybe one day – who can tell? – maybe one day you'll come back into my arms without your famous historical laws.

She makes a gesture such as I cannot describe. She simply adjusts her head, so that I can see her hair and the nape of her neck.

Supposing you had to choose an epitaph? she asks.

If I had to chose an epitaph, I'd choose *The Polish Rider*, I tell her.

You can't choose a painting as an epitaph!

I can't?

It's wonderful when there's somebody to pull off your boots for you. 'She knows how to get his boots off' is a proverbial Russian compliment. I pull off my own tonight. And, once off, being motorbike boots, they stand apart. They are different, not because they have metal in certain places as a protection, nor because they have an added piece of leather near the toecap so that they resist the wear and tear of flicking the gear pedal up, nor because they have a phosphorescent sign around the calf so that the rider is more visible at night in the headlights of the vehicle behind, but because, pulling them off, I have the feeling of stepping to the side of the many thousands of kilometres we have ridden together, they and I. They could be the seven-league boots that so fascinated me as a child. The boots I wanted to take everywhere with me, for even then I was dreaming of roads, although the road made me shit-scared.

I love the painting of the Polish Rider as a child might, for it is the beginning of a story being told by an old man who has seen many things and never wants to go to bed.

I love the rider as a woman might: his nerve, his insolence, his vulnerability, the strength of his thighs. Liz is right. Many horses course through dreams here.

In 1939 units of Polish cavalry armed with swords charged against the tanks of the invading Panzer divisions. In the seventeenth century, the 'Winged Horsemen' were feared as the avenging angels of the eastern plains. Yet the horse means more than military prowess. Over the centuries Poles have been continually obliged to travel or emigrate. Across their land without natural frontiers the roads never end.

The equestrian habit is still sometimes visible in bodies and the way they move. The gesture of putting the right foot in a stirrup and hoicking the other leg over comes to my mind whilst sitting in a pizza bar in Warsaw watching men and women who have never in their lives mounted or even touched a horse, and who are drinking Pepsi-cola.

I love the Polish Rider's horse as a horseman who has lost his mount and has been given another might. The gift horse is a bit long in the tooth – the Poles call such a nag a *szkapa* – but he's an animal whose loyalty has been proven.

Finally I love the landscape's invitation, wherever it may lead.

It has led to the village of Górecko in the south-east of what is named Little Poland, twenty kilometres from the Ukrainian border.

The village street is dust and stones. There are two shops, and along an overgrown path through the forest, a church. In the centre of the village, near a shrine to the Madonna, where wild asparagus grows in the spring, there is a small reservoir full of green water. The villagers dug and built the reservoir in the 1960s as part of a miniature hydro-electric plan drawn up by the local priest to bring electricity to the village. It didn't work, but the fact that the Church was meddling with the formula *Soviets + Electricity = Communism* forced the authorities to supply the area, perhaps more quickly than they would otherwise have done, from the national grid system. Today, when a workhorse goes mad, the villagers stand the animal in the reservoir for several hours, until the animal cools down.

The houses are mostly wooden *chatas* of two rooms with a stove between them (in winter the temperature can be −20° C) and a chimney in the middle of the roof. The four small windows are doubled – there's often a pot-plant placed lovingly in the space between the two frames. The gardens are surrounded by wooden fences and in them grow beetroots, cabbages, potatoes, leeks. Some *chatas* have been enlarged, rebuilt, fitted with radiators, and given a portico with wooden columns. The plot of land, though, is still the same plot, and the money for improving the grandparents' house has been earnt in Germany or Chicago.

My friend Mirek's house stands apart from the village on the other side of the main road. For the last seven years Mirek has worked, as an illegal migrant, on building sites in Paris. By training he is a forestry engineer. I have learnt much from him in the forest.

Normally he walks fast, in the same way that he drives cars fast. He doesn't take risks, for he's aware there are too many anyway. With his large hands and shoulders, he's not somebody you would think of push-ing aside. His eyes, though, are unexpected, for in them there is a reflective, almost hesitant, questioning. Is it this questioning which explains his success with women? We need to make promises, he told me one day, without promises life is too hard for anybody, but if you make a promise you don't believe in, it's not a promise! Maybe this is why he prefers actions to words. As I say, he normally walks fast.

On that particular morning, he had reduced his pace and from time to time squatted to examine the earth between the pine trees. I want to show you the Lion of the Ants, he said, there ought to be one here. A sort of ant? No, a larva, a grub. About the size of a fingernail. When he gets wings he's like a dragonfly, and silvery like satin. The soil between the pines where he was looking was sandy and in the sunlight. He couldn't find one.

He approached a tree stump and touched the sticky, cut wood. Just the place for *oprinka miodowa*. They're a mushroom, he said, that taste of the deep forest. If they knew how to cook, the wild boar would eat them! Boil them for a moment to get rid of a certain bitterness – don't include the stalks, they're slender but stringy – and serve them with fresh cream! He said this smiling. What makes Mirek smile most frequently is the pleasure of outwitting the routines and tired rules of daily life, and when his smile gets too big, he breaks into laughter. He has the eye and imagination of a poacher.

We walked on in silence for half an hour. Abruptly he stopped in his tracks, knelt and pointed at a small crater in the sand, the diameter of a saucer. It was shaped like a funnel that got narrower and narrower.

See his head and pincers? He's hiding there in the sand, waiting for the next ant to slide down the funnel into his mouth! The Lion of Ants! He begins, Mirek explained, by making a circle on the ground, he makes it walking backwards – he can't walk forwards because his hind legs have evolved into diggers. The sand he extracts he shovels aside with a quick toss of his head. Then he makes a second circle, a little narrower and a little deeper. And he goes on like this, circle after circle, till he's at the bottom, where he hides. Once an ant lurches into that shifting sand, he can't help himself. When he hasn't eaten for days and is very hungry, the Lion will draw a wide circle so that more ants fall down the slope for him to eat. When he's not so hungry, he draws a small circle. He writes his menu on the sand!

Mirek's smile broke into laughter, then he looked up at the sky above the trees as if to acknowledge the mystery of why things have come to be exactly the way they are.

There is no other house like Mirek's. Probably one can say that about any house if one knows it well enough. Anyway I know what to expect. I follow the grass track which leads off the road, I cross the bridge, made of wooden planks, over the stream, I pass the tree to the left of the door with apples the size and colour of dark cherries (incredibly bitter to taste), and I look for the key in my pocket. There are no steps leading to the front door – one has to step up fifty centimetres on to a concrete platform. The wooden door has two locks which I undo. It doesn't open. Putting my fingers under the bevel of one of its panels, I succeed in lifting it. The door yields and swings open. I step in. The house smells of dust, wood-smoke and fern. I wander from room to room – there are six. In each there is at least one butterfly or moth, either flying around calmly, or fluttering its wings against a windowpane with the fast flicking sound of a banknote counting-machine.

The house was built more than a century ago. Only three of the eight dining chairs don't collapse when sat upon. There is an image of the Madonna in every room. Nobody is clear about the house's exact history, or perhaps everybody wants to forget a different chapter of its history. Doubtless it has served many purposes. The unhidden electrical circuit, with its wires, sockets, connections, points, fuses and switches all tacked to the walls, looks as if it was improvised in great haste, to meet some emergency forty years ago. Perhaps when electricity first came to the village?

Fix it! From next week we're operating from here – day and night, summer and winter, understood? There'll always be just one of us here. So fix it, you've got till Monday.

Or could it be that the house then belonged to an old woman living far away, one of whose local nephews, when the electricity came, seized the chance to pretend to be an electrician, and in exchange for the work done, demanded enough money to buy himself a mobylette?

I switch on the electricity. I put the bacon and the *śmietanie* I have brought with me on the kitchen table. I've promised to have some soup ready for them when they arrive. Within an hour and a half there'll be hot water.

At about the same moment as the electricity was

installed, the windows were changed. There are many more of them and they are far larger than they could have been originally. What lay behind this mania for windows?

A step towards modernity or another proposal by the nephew to the old woman? Unlike installing the electricity, creating and enlarging the windows must have taken many months of work and he would have earnt himself enough for a small second-hand car.

Or was it a Committee Decision?

If there's plenty of light, we'll use less electricity. No problem with getting the window frames, they'll be delivered direct from the factory. Proceed room by room, we'll be occupying the others! OK?

Only three of the twenty double window frames now open. Several have been painted over and are opaque, and a number have been broken and the panes of glass replaced by sheets of polystyrene. There are no curtains.

In the larder, which is a blind passage with a door leading off the kitchen (there is no refrigerator), I find a bottle of beer. It was brewed in the village of Zwierzyniec, which means place of the animals, twelve kilometres from here. I take the bottle into one of the front rooms where there is an armchair.

On the wall hang a pair of stag antlers, and opposite them an old framed photo of a hunter with shotgun and dog. The photo is difficult to date. Mirek doesn't know who the man is. Probably at one time he was living here.

The antlers are in fact a joke: they are branches of a

spruce, hung on the wall to give the impression of a pair of antlers.

Liane is a Romanian painter. She sent me a drawing she had made in the Berlin Natural History Museum. It showed a large tree trunk, with real antlers growing out of it on each side. She explained that a stag must have one day died beside the roots of a young tree, which subsequently grew around its skull and lifted them up and preserved them. I told friends who were going to Berlin to go to the museum and look at it and I showed them her drawing. Each reported back to me that they could find no such exhibit. Finally I asked Liane. Of course, she said, smiling, only I can find it. We'll have to go to the museum together, maybe it's gone now.

The hunter in the photo is wearing a cap. Today baseball caps, as worn by the young all over the world, with the peak pointing backwards, have superseded the traditional cap with its polished peak and its particular claims. The claims of the Polish cap were: an indestructible patriotism; a right to command; a willingness to serve; a familiarity with nature and all her extremes; a gift for secrecy and for bargaining; a very long experience of history.

Anybody could buy and wear such a cap. It was a

thousand times easier than acquiring a passport. During the nineteenth century, when occupied Poland did not exist as a nation, the wearing of this cap bestowed and preserved a strange authority. The hunter in the photo might have been able to explain the mystery of the tree with the antlers.

A few minutes' walk away from the house, there is another mystery. In the forest, surrounded by undergrowth and with no path leading to it, there's a grave – well-kept, with a bouquet of artificial flowers placed on it. A soldier of the German Wehrmacht was buried there sixty years ago. And the bouquet is renewed every few months.

The soldier was shot on 31 December 1943 in this house. Perhaps he was actually shot outside near the apple tree with apples the size of cherries, but the decision to shoot him was taken here. The impulse which led to the act began in this room – perhaps decision is too unconfused a word. The German was barely eighteen years old. He had been conscripted at sixteen, and after a few weeks' training was posted to the occupying army in this area. His name was Hans. After a few months he announced to a forester, whom he met secretly, that he wanted to desert from the Wehrmacht and join the Polish partisans. Some say he had fallen in love with a girl in the village, who lived in the house next to the one where the second shop now is. The girl, when she became an old woman and Hans was mentioned, would shake her head in such a manner that it was hard to be sure whether she was confirming or denying the story. Many weeks passed after Hans spoke to the forester. He was cross-questioned several times by two officers from the A.K., the clandestine partisan Army of the Interior, whose allegiance was not to the Russians but to the exiled Polish government in London. The partisan command had doubts about him. Eventually he was told he could work as a medical orderly in their forest hospital if he handed over his uniform, papers and rifle. He agreed. One of the wounded in the hospital began to teach him the rudiments of Polish.

On the night in question Hans accompanied, at their invitation, the A.K. colonel and several section commanders who came to the village, and more particularly to this house, to celebrate the New Year of 1944.

What happened after many vodkas is obscure. Did Hans, forgetting himself, start to hum a German song? Did he receive a message from the girl and try to slip out of the house, by the door in the kitchen, without saying a word? He was making progress with his Polish. Or did the colonel suffer a sudden vision of imminent betrayal?

He knows far more about us than we know about him. We don't even know whether or not he can be trusted.

At that time one killing superseded another and thousands occurred simultaneously. On 1 June the entire population, including babies and grandparents, of a village twelve kilometres from here had been massacred by the German SS. The previous year 400,000 Jews had been rounded up and interned in the Warsaw ghetto to be dispatched to the extermination camps. In February 1943, the British government had taken the decision to give priority to the fire-bombing of enemy cities so as 'to destroy the morale of the enemy civilian population'.

A killing could provoke a momentary recoil, a second of confusion, but scarcely a regret. I doubt whether Hans fully realised what was happening when he was shot in the back of the neck, where the apple tree with the bitter fruit now grows. No struggle. Four men carried him into the forest and buried him. His corpse benefited from the doubt that he was perhaps not an enemy.

The mystery, though, concerns his grave not his death. In the early 1950s a wooden cross was suddenly planted at its head. No name, no date. Years later a stainless steel screw replaced the rusty original one which held the cross together. And always, laid on the mound of the grave, there is a bouquet of artificial flowers, while twenty metres away in the undergrowth lie the tatters, like confetti, of the discarded bouquets.

Everyone in the village knows who is doing this. The old woman who shook her head is dead. Yet the grave receives more regular attention than most graves in tended cemeteries. Is this because the attention given to it is secret, and, at the same time, acknowledged by all those who remember?

I once questioned an old villager about the grave. His

reply was fox-like. A man died there, he said, so what could be more natural than to mark the place?

Paradoxically, a memory of a moment of confusion can be unconfused. Sitting in the armchair between the joke antlers and the photo of the hunter with his cap, such a memory comes to me. It is not mine, this memory of the impulse in this room to kill Hans sixty years ago. I decide it's time to go and pick the sorrel for the soup I'm going to make.

In the open air the distinction between the kingdoms – mineral, vegetable, animal – seems blurred. There are leaves, curled up with dryness on the wooden planks of the bridge, which look like toads. A hornet on a sunflower – there's a nest of hornets in the attic – could be mistaken for one of its seeds. I sit on the planks of the bridge, my legs dangling over the water, and watch the stream. The water is a little lower than usual because the mill upstream is working. When it stops at night or at lunchtime, the water rises by twenty centimetres. The mill turns an old circular saw, which cuts the trunks of pine trees into new planks. During the next ten years, in the forest to the north, where Despina was accepted by the wolves, it is being planned that one and a half million trees will be cut down and sold for quick profit. Not only the level of the water can change, but also its colour. This afternoon it is clear. At other times the stream is turgid and dark, the colour of water in a bowl in which dried mushrooms have been soaked. Why is sand seen through water so inviting? The stream has influenced the growth of every tree growing along its two banks, and a number of them are far older than the house. On the stream's surface the traces of its current, and the circular ripples caused by the interruption of a stone or a fallen branch, remind me of cable stitching. Knit three, purl three . . . I remember the needles.

As well as the blurring of the distinction between the three kingdoms, the distinction between past and present has become blurred. Here the river is called the *Szum*; there it was called the *Ching*.

The Ching flowed at the bottom of the small suburban garden of the house I lived in until I was six, in Highams Park, a downmarket east London suburb, twenty minutes by train from Liverpool Street. In the garden there was golden rod and pampas grass. There were also gooseberries and marigolds, the latter planted by my mother for they were her favourite flower. In Spanish the marigold is called *maravilla*, which means wonder, and in Mexico it is the flower of the great carnival of Death. Across the Ching, which, like the Szum, is about three metres wide, there was a draw-bridge built by my father for me. Every Saturday afternoon when he didn't go to the office, we went down to the bridge, which stood vertical on our bank, and lowered it, through a system of ropes and pulleys, until it was horizontal and rested on the opposite bank. Then we could cross with dry feet to the other side. Like the one I'm sitting on, the bridge in Highams Park was made of planks, and one could see the water between them, but it was much narrower, it was only as wide as my two five-year-old arms held out sideways. The bridge led nowhere. On the opposite bank was a field of allotments with a fence round it. We crossed simply to be on the other side, and to look back.

The Ching was my father's river. For a few years it was the best thing in his life, and he wanted to share it with me. It cleaned the remembered wounds that would never heal. It dispersed the mustard gas. With lips wet like the Szum's, it whispered names. (After the war ended in 1918, my father, who had served four years as an infantry captain, served for two more years in Flanders on the War Graves Commission.) The Ching could not bring back any of the countless dead but he could cross over the drawbridge to the other side and stand there for a minute or two, as if he were the man of twenty-five who in 1913 could not imagine a single hour of the four years of trench warfare to come.

When he lowered the drawbridge, he could borrow my innocence and so recall his own, which otherwise – except for those Saturday afternoons – was for ever lost.

All this, at the age of four and a half, or five, as I lay on my stomach and let the water of the Ching flow around my wrists, I knew in my blood. My dark blood.

Those Saturday afternoons were the beginning of an undertaking my father and I shared until he died, and which now I continue alone.

By the time I was ten and until he was seventy, he and I contested one another almost continually. There were truces during which we both abstained, yet they were rare and brief. Everything I did alarmed him about my future. Everything he believed in I wanted to overturn. He was trying to save me – to crawl out on his belly to a crater in no-man's-land and pull me back to relative safety – and I, with all the arrogance and fear of youth, was trying to show him that it was possible to be what I called free.

The fights were sometimes cruel and bitter and both of us were reckless. He wept more often than I, because the wounds I inflicted opened up older ones, whereas those he inflicted on me provoked the protective indignation that often accompanies youthful revolt. Nevertheless, throughout this long struggle, our mutual undertaking, which began wordlessly with the drawbridge over the Ching and which would never be openly declared, was never lost sight of and persisted. (I'm writing this with a worn pencil whose marks are so faint that I cannot reread the words in the evening light, for what I'm saying, twenty-five years after his death, can still only be said in a whisper.) And it consisted of what, this undertaking? An agreement that he could share with me, as he could share with nobody else, the ghost life of his four years of trench warfare, and that he could do so because I already knew them; they were, in the strictest sense of the term, familiar to me.

We fought about my future with no holds barred and no exchanges possible, yet neither of us forgot for a second during the fight that we shared the secrets of another incommensurable war. By being himself, my father taught me endurance. By being myself, I reminded him that he was not alone.

The Saturday afternoons were very long. Time seemed mercifully to stop. Lying here on the planks of the wide bridge over the Szum and closing my eyes, the sound of the two streams merge, along with the sound of the midges, of the distant dog barking, of the leaves of the tall trees. And in the current of the two streams there is the same indifference.

My father had a pair of wading boots that he wore when he was standing in the water attending to the bridge. The water, deeper than I was tall, came up to the tops of his thighs. My mother came down to the river bank only when the gooseberries were ripe and she wanted to make jam. Otherwise, like pubs, betting-shops and billiard parlours, it was a strictly male area, measuring about ten metres by four.

One Saturday I found a wading boot and stepped in with both feet; it came up to my head, it covered me and I hopped along the bank in it, laughing. My father laughed too. All of me was in one of his boots. And I knew where he had been in other boots. And he knew I knew whilst we laughed together.

On 18th March 1917 he wrote in a letter to his father: I stood a moment wondering whether I ought to take thirty men through such an Inferno; just then my Sergeant came up from the dug-out and shouting into my ear at the top of his voice to make himself heard through the crash of guns and the bursting of the shells, he said, 'Excuse me, Sir, we will go through hell with you, Sir, if you're thinking of us.' That settled it. I would go. We start out into the open – we are lucky at first – their machine guns open on us and we jump into a trench – we are up to our waists in water – our ammunition is all wet – but still we plod along – the guns never ceasing for a solitary moment.

We met stragglers coming back – some lost, some wounded, and many lay dead. Not knowing whether we could eventually get through, I shouted to my Sergeant to take charge and push on as fast as possible and I would try to go on in advance and see if the way was clear. My servant came with me and one other man. I then met an artillery officer who had lost his reason; it appeared that he could not get in touch with the infantry and he didn't know whether his battery was shooting on trenches occupied by ourselves or the Hun. He blew out his brains with his revolver in front of my eyes.

My men got stuck in the clayey trench and it took me one and a half hours to dig them out. My last drop of water was expended on a man who was wounded in ten places.

A woman with a white scarf around her head is approaching the bridge over the Szum, carrying two buckets full of freshly dug potatoes. When just taken from the earth, potatoes glow. They glow like hen's eggs. The woman is perspiring. I recognise her from my other visits. She is Bogena, who looks after Mirek's garden and, in exchange, takes the vegetables and flowers she needs. Due to the river, the soil is richer here than in the village proper across the road. And so Bogena keeps chickens in her own garden and cultivates Mirek's. In the room where I'll be sleeping, I'll hear, far away, her cock crowing before it is light.

Scrambling to my feet, I ask whether I can have five or six potatoes. I'm thinking of the soup. Bogena puts down her buckets and takes my hands and pulls them out in front of me. Then she places potatoes in them, one by one, until I can hold no more. I am nearly twice her age yet the way she does this somehow refers to the child in me.

If the river at the bottom of the garden in Gordon Avenue was my father's happiness, mine was the house next door. It did not have a front door like the others in the road, but a side door, two metres away from the outside wall of our own house. This door was seldom locked. Front doors are by definition locked. I could slip into the house next door whenever I wanted.

The door opened on to a small panelled room with a curved wooden ceiling which must have been added on to the original house, and perhaps once served as a drying room for the washing. Now its shape, its wood, and the fact that there was nothing in it except a bench against the wall and a low table, made it seem like an upturned boat. There was a window – in the stern – which gave on to the back garden where there was a pear tree. In the month of November, the low table in the upturned boat was covered with pears, carefully placed in rows, no two pears touching, by the man of the house.

On the bench was a cushion which slowly over the years became mine. Their kitchen led out of the boat-room and the door was often open, so I sat and heard their voices talking in their language. Sometimes their dog, an Airedale who came up to my shoulder, would be lying on the floor and I would stroke him. He had wiry hair that smelt of a kind of tobacco. I have forgotten his name. If I could remember it, I'd be able to re-enter another room. On other days I looked at the pictures in the papers or books that had been left on the bench. Some of the books were children's books, yet there was no child in the house. The daughter, tall and with very black hair, was in her teens, finishing her schooling.

The mother noticed when I came in and let me be.

Sometimes there was music playing on the wind-up gramophone in the sitting room, where the father, who was out of work, read newspapers. What enticed me to the house next door, whenever I could slip away, was the pleasure of waiting. The pleasure of waiting a long, long while with the certainty that, at the end, I would not be forgotten.

Finally, the mother, with her kerchief tied very high around her head, would bring me, from the kitchen, if it was the afternoon, a saucer with a cinnamon cake on it and a cup of hot chocolate. If it was the morning, a pot of home-made yoghurt. At that time, in the early thirties, yoghurt — except amongst health-food freaks — was entirely unknown in London. She never kissed me. She looked at me kindly from a considerable distance. She treated me as if I had a mission in life which she knew about and prayed that I would fulfil. Perhaps the mission was just to grow up and become a man.

Only Camellia, their daughter, spoke English easily. She took me on expeditions into Epping Forest. She showed me how animals die: It's fallen, it'll never leave the ground again. We both had knives for cutting. Tendrils, bines and worts. What she showed me was a secret. We might have explained, when asked, where we had been; we would never tell what we had seen.

I did a drawing of an owl and together we hid it in the hollow of an oak tree that had been split by lightning. When we returned the next week the drawing had gone and the hollow was full of feathers. We collected the feathers and

Camellia said we could write with them. I thought she meant they were an alphabet. It could be that it is with them that I'm writing at this moment.

Camellia's family came from somewhere in the Austro-Hungarian Empire, which, until the end of the First World War, included this bridge over the river Szum. I never found out exactly what disaster had forced them to emigrate. All I took in was their homesickness and the various ways they possessed of combating it – tisanes, sachets of dried lavender, records of Liszt, cheesecake, dried mushrooms, a certain way of pulling on their socks. Whatever their story – it was not a Jewish one – the father had been dishonoured in some way, this I could feel, and this was why he gazed into the middle distance and spoke rarely. He was waiting for a message to come which would rectify the error. It never, of course, came.

I walk towards the field where the wild sorrel grows. I have left Bogena's potatoes in a small pile on the planks of the bridge where they are glowing like eggs. I cut the sorrel plants with my pocket knife. They are about the size of young dandelions, but the green of their leaves, like their taste, is both sweeter and more acid. They grow in clumps together, so I sit down and spread out my handkerchief on the grass and place the cut leaves on it.

The pictorial convention of using fig leaves to hide the human genitalia is comic – the leaves are too shiny and too heraldic. Wild sorrel plants would be far more appropriate, for their leaves feel like green skin when you touch them. Exactly like green skin. Exactly. I've picked enough and I remain sitting.

There are no birds to be seen. The sporadic, loud trilling comes from between the leaves of the surrounding trees and bushes. I have the impression it is the foliage itself that is singing! I remember having the same sensation in Gordon Avenue. The two moments, instead of being separated by decades, belong to the same hour of the same season. I wipe and close the knife.

A kind of vertigo overcomes me. Words make no more sense. Everything is a continuum.

You asked me, Juan, to write something for you about pocket knives, pocket knives and boyhood. I told you I thought pocket knives went with torches. A knife in one pocket and a torch in the other! I never got round to writing anything. Then unaccountably you died.

You are looking at me sardonically, as I hoped you would. Listen, here's a knife story!

I've held this knife in my hand and it was made in the village of Josefow. I've seen the grave of the man who made it. A very proud man by all accounts. He was a craftsman, perhaps a harness-maker or a saddler.

He had three children, two boys and a girl, who was the youngest. Either because he knew she was probably his last child, or because of her fierce blue eyes and dark hair, or for his own reasons, he loved her particularly.

This was in 1906, when everyone in Poland was waiting to see what would happen next, after the revolts and strikes of the previous year. The historians would later call it a revolution.

The protests across the country had been about poverty, hunger, working conditions, and most of all about the Polish language, which was forbidden to be taught in any school, or used for any official purpose. The Russians, Prussians and Austrians who occupied the country wanted the language suppressed. Many men and women died in pools of blood fighting for the right to their own words. To die for a certain declension. A certain declension and certain names! The daughter's name was Eva and her birthday was in May.

After giving the matter considerable thought, the father decided that his birthday present should be a pocket knife, which he would make, especially for her, in his workshop. He had noticed how she was always pestering one of her brothers to lend her his pocket knife.

Her knife should be small, not more than nine centimetres long when shut, and seventeen centimetres when open. The handle should be made from a ram horn, honey-grey, slightly translucent. He would find one at Romek's store in Aleksandrow, split it, and with four brass rivets attach the two halves to the steel spine, slightly curved, mounting towards the tail. The steel blade would also curve and narrow to a point.

The father made it. The knife is small and feminine – like a barrette for a massive head of black hair. When shut, if you hold it in your right hand, the blade of the knife glints like a moon in its final phase after the last quarter. It's small, but one could gut a trout with it, peel a pear, cut wild sorrel, open a letter, remove a stone from a goat's cleft hoof – if the goat was calm. The knife, however, has one peculiarity.

Who knows at what moment during its making the father made his decision. Was it when he first imagined the knife? Or was it only towards the end, after he had made the handle, and before he fitted the blade that is held by a single clamping pin?

The peculiarity of the knife is that the cutting edge of the blade is as thick and as rounded as its back edge. It is a knife perfectly made *not* to cut. It has a cancelled blade. At the beginning of the twentieth century, in the year 1906, when revolutions and troops firing into crowds were the order of the day throughout central and eastern Europe, a man made a knife like this so that his beloved Eva would be less likely to cut her finger.

When you open it, Juan, it occurs to you it's a Hamlet-object you're holding. It contains a recognised desire and, running parallel, the fear which that desire provokes. A knife of indecision. Open or shut, the blade is always one of regret.

Yet is that all? This Hamlet-object, which has survived its century against all the odds, speaks of something else:

of the wish that a loved one has everything, but everything!

I decide to pull two leeks from the vegetable garden. I need a fork because the earth has baked hard. There should be a fork in the portico, along with an axe and a pick. I find it, pull the leeks, and shake the parched earth out of their white roots. The leeks smell of violets and nickel.

Back in the house, I go into the room next to the one where the hunter and antlers are to wind up the clock that is there and set it at the right hour. There's a piece of furniture in this room the like of which I'd never seen until I came here.

Probably it hasn't been used as it was intended to be for close on a century. On the odd drunken night women may have teased men with it. Perhaps, once, a woman climbed on to it naked and the men gasped as she went higher and higher. Otherwise it stood there unused and untouched. And, although it takes up a good deal of space – on the floor it covers an area of one metre by three metres and it's over two metres tall – nobody has thought of dismantling it. To do so would be easy, a question of undoing a dozen nuts.

It commands a kind of awe; it has a precision and lightness which imply that it was imagined with great care and then patiently constructed according to detailed drawings. It's made of slender lengths of polished beech wood, and its form is that of the letter A, except that it's in three dimensions – or four if one includes the rhythm of its soaring.

It is a swing, an indoor swing. The seat of polished slats (the horizontal stroke of the A) is high off the ground. It was made not for a child but for a woman, perhaps when she announced she was going to have a baby. A throne, a rocking chair, a nursing seat, a swing, a perch. I undo the cord attachment and gently push the seat. It soars, comes back, soars . . . I hear the clock ticking. I remember the first time I was here and how I helped Mirek move the swing from the room where we ate into this room with a bed in it. I remember how he looked at the swing when we had placed it in its new position. He looked at it as if it were a relic.

Mirek has the talents of both poacher and innkeeper (the lean and the well-fed man) and these serve him well for the clandestine jobs he finds and performs in Paris: building chimneys, laying tiles, constructing verandas, mending roofs, installing central heating systems, building duplex apartments, or repainting a bedroom with a specially chosen colour, for Parisians. He is strong with sharp eyes and the methodical intelligence of an engineer. He has something else too, his own way of planning each job, for no two jobs are the same.

When he was at school and living in his mother's small house in Zamość, his mother's brother, Zanek, lived with them. Zanek was almost totally paralysed. He could not speak and he noticed everything!

Everything – that's why I loved him. After school I would go and talk with him, for we invented a language between us, a language like no other, neither Polish nor Russian, nor Lithuanian, nor French, nor German, a language in which we could say what nobody else said; maybe every love invents a vocabulary, a cover to shelter under. With him I discovered something I've never forgotten.

Zanek spent the days alone in the house in Zamość because his sister went to work. Before she left, she arranged the day's newspaper for him. He read everything in it and couldn't turn the page. In December 1970 Polish soldiers in Gdansk were ordered to fire on Polish workers, who were on strike in protest against rising prices and the lack of food, and that morning Zanek asked his sister to leave the radio on. Usually his days were silent.

Mirek pondered all this while he was at school. He started making diagrams and eventually he built a radio with a control system whose switches his uncle, lying immobile on the bed, could operate with his nose!

No two jobs are the same.

In Paris Mirek learnt how to work and remain unnoticed – taking a painter's ladder out of a car or dumping sacks of gravel into a street container at the wrong moment can lead to questions and speedy repatriation.

He discovered where to buy materials and to pay for everything on the spot with cash. He got used to insisting in his elementary French and not answering back, listening, waiting and making certain that he was paid as promised. With the money he earnt and hid away, he dreamt of what he would one day build at home. He bought, after five years in Paris, a two-roomed flat in Warsaw. He had further dreams. He became another Polish Rider but older. Meanwhile he lived with what fitted into two suitcases and with a few dozen Polish songs, including several that his uncle loved to listen to on the radio.

I give the swing another push. It goes high, and when it returns, soars as high as my head.

In Paris women fell in love with Mirek – Polish women who, after many tribulations, had settled abroad to earn a living independently, or pursue their careers. Some fell in love with him for a second time, for they had known him when he was a student. He took them fishing on the Marne at night. He cooked borsch for them. They spent whole Sundays in bed. They watched satellite Polish TV. When they were with him, it was as if he stopped danger existing.

One by one, each did her best to persuade him to join her in Germany, in Switzerland, in Houston, USA, and stay for good. There are more Poles in Chicago than in any other city of the world after Warsaw. These women had sustained their courage alone and they knew they must refuse to look back: only look ahead. They still loved eating ice cream. And each, in her own way, sharply wanted Mirek at her side. None of them, however, could contemplate returning with him to Poland and having children who would go to school and fall in love there, and in their turn have to leave and say goodbye. Mirek, each one of them told him in her own words, you're my dream, but you don't understand women!

And so, two years ago, Mirek looked at the swing as if it were a relic.

A knock on the door. No vehicle has drawn up. I cross the porch whose broken windows have been replaced with dark polystyrene panels and open the sagging door. Bogena is holding out a bowl of eggs. For the sorrel soup, she says. Bogena, except for regular errands to Zamość and the occasional visit to Lublin, has never left the village. This is evident in the way she observes me standing in the doorway of this house she has always known. The uninhabited and visited house. The house without a doorstep. I thank her and she turns away, walking at a pace that hasn't changed for years.

I peel and slice the potatoes and cut the bacon into small pieces and wash the leeks. Their outer leaves pull off like satin sleeves and the ones disclosed glisten. Towards their heads, earth, as it always does, has infiltrated between the skins, so I make a short vertical cut and flicker through the skins like pages and wash out the irritating dirt. Cutting the leeks into round slices, the knife makes a ratchet noise, which is one of the oldest sounds I remember.

Four days ago, Mirek married Danka. They'll be here in an hour.

Danka was born in Nowy Targ in Galicia. Under socialism there was a shoe factory in the small town employing over three thousand workers. It was the country's largest shoe factory, established there because of the long-standing local tradition of working with skins and hides from the cattle of the nearby Carpathian Mountains. Now the factory is closed and the town poor. Nobody starves in Nowy Targ as they do in Milano or Paris, but there's a pall of silence over the town for there are no projects to discuss. The town lives, like dust, from day to day. And its six or seven taxis wait discreetly, just off the main square, for the occasional fare, usually a foreigner. Danka is the youngest of five children. Her father worked in the factory. Her aunt has two cows.

She left Nowy Targ nine years ago, at the age of eighteen, to go to Paris where she eventually found work as a maid. Paid like a cleaner, she in fact brought up the two children of her employers, who leased her a small room above the garage where they kept their cars. There she slept and there the children – when they were old enough – sneaked in to hear bedtime stories. Within a couple of years Danka spoke a fluent French.

Mirek met Danka on a Friday night, her night off, at a birthday party of a mutual Polish friend in Paris.

I'm turning the leeks and the bacon and the potatoes in a frying pan, and I'm inventing their love story.

They both noticed one another that first evening. He was fifteen years older than she. She noticed how he talked. He talked like a horseman who had studied at some distant university, but she was not intimidated. He noticed her shoulders, neck and mouth; they shared a kind of insistence, the insistence of a goose in flight. At one moment he put his hand on her shoulder and she responded without a word. She spoke little; she preferred her thoughts to be read. At the end of the evening he offered her a lift home in his car, and on the way she told him about the children she was looking after, and he told her about his flat in Warsaw. Into the car stereo he put a CD of the Warsaw group, Budka Suflera (Prompter's Box).

When they reached her employer's house, the car stopped, but she didn't get out, and the car turned round to go to the other side of Paris where Mirek had his room.

Red poppies already here
beloved body already sore
to our foreheads apply
the cool salt of Wieliczka.

The next time they met, they showed one another photographs and he cooked for her.

Where did you learn to cook so well?

I've been teaching myself for twenty years.

She said it would be better if he slept with her in her room for then they wouldn't have to get up so early.

And the *patronne*? he asked.

I pay her rent for my room, she said, you can sleep in my bed all day long if you like.

I'm slipping everything from the frying pan into a saucepan of salted, boiling water.

After two weeks Danka announced that, ideally, she would like to have at least two children.

Two?

One after the other, quick, so you're not too old!

Me too old!

Not now – but in ten years when you're teaching them

203

to fish, or when you're climbing Mount Trzy Korony
with them for the first time!

Have you climbed it?

With my brother when I was a kid. We saw some
mouflon. Ouch! Men never get used to undoing hooks.
Let me.

I'm cutting up the sorrel leaves with my pocket knife. Finely
and not too finely. It should look like green confetti.

When it was confirmed that she was one and a half
months pregnant, they agreed to get married after the
baby was born.

In a few weeks we'll know, he said, whether it's a boy
or a girl.

A wedding in Nowy Targ! she said. No, she wouldn't
dream of getting married in Paris!

In Paris they will buy a wedding dress.

Choosing a wedding dress is unlike choosing any other
garment. The bride, when dressed, has to appear to have
come from a place where nobody present has ever been,
because it is the place of her own name. The woman to be

married becomes Bride the moment she is transformed into a stranger. A stranger so that the man she is marrying can recognise her as if for the first time; a stranger so she can be surprised, at the moment when they make their vows, by the man she is marrying. Why are brides ritually hidden before the ceremony? It is to facilitate the transformation whereby the bride appears to have come from the other side of a horizon. The veil is the veil of that distance. A woman who has lived her whole life in the same village walks down the aisle of her village church as a bride, and to all those watching she becomes, for an instant, unrecognisable, not because she is wearing a disguise, but because she has become a newcomer being greeted on arrival.

Danka, after much delicious hesitation, chose her dress of arrival. It had a scooped neckline, bare shoulders with lace trimming, a sheath bodice with a thousand silver threads, and a satin skirt with flounces and twelve white roses of organza. It cost the equivalent of four months of her wages. Don't think twice, Mirek said. A Parisian dress in lace and satin and with flounces as wide as a bed – selling it when we get to Warsaw will be child's play!

So we can leave it to Olek? she asked. By now they knew she was carrying a boy.

Their plan was to move into the flat in Warsaw, which they would later exchange for a slightly larger one. Mirek would start a business installing bathrooms, jacuzzis, saunas, etc. He didn't want to work like a mule on building sites any more; he'd become an ablutions specialist. And in the larger flat, when they found it, Danka would run a nursery looking after other babies as well as her own.

I put on the eggs to boil. From over the shallow sink to above where the logs are stacked beside the kitchen stove runs a clothes line for drying linen. Since the house has been empty for months, nothing is drying on it; all that hangs there is a soup ladle whose bowl has been reworked and pinched together in such a way that it has a throat and a lip to pour from; it has been transformed into an improbable multipurpose utensil for distributing soup, serving custard, and pouring steaming jam into pots. In one of the stories I do not know of this house without women, men too must have made jam.

Olek weighed 4.2 kilos at birth. He was delivered in a hospital in the nineteenth arrondissement of Paris. Danka's employers arranged for her to have papers and a work permit so that she wouldn't have to leave them before they found someone reliable to replace her. She's irreplaceable! said the man. Everyone is replaceable, said the woman.

When Danka returned to her room above the garage, the expression of plenitude on her face had not diminished.

Instead of listening to herself, she listened, day and night, to the sounds that came from her boy. Within a week she restarted work, taking Olek everywhere with her. The daughter of the house, aged five, declared she wanted a baby. A baby like him. She was watching Danka breastfeed Olek. After she said this, she let her head fall against Danka's shoulder, as if sharing the worries of motherhood.

Amongst their Polish friends in Paris, Olek was passed from hand to hand, the men's hands often swollen or bruised, roughened by cement, the women's hands sometimes over pink as if over-licked from the incessant work of ironing and washing. Everyone agreed that the baby looked like Mirek, the same wide hands, the same blue-grey eyes. And look! Look! He has the same ears. Perhaps Mirek, with a father's pride, was trying to look like his son.

Were I to have another life, born on another continent, there would, I believe, be one kind of gathering which, should I ever come across it, I would unerringly identify as Polish, even if I didn't know where Poland was!

A small room. People seated on chairs, a stool, a click-clack bed, backs to the wall. In the middle of the crowded, small room, on the floor, a baby asleep in a carrycot. They are talking, knitting, telling stories, cutting a sausage, discussing prices, yet the gaze of them all repeatedly returns to the carrycot as if it were a fire whose flames draw their attention. Every so often one of them gets up to look closely at the baby. The fire has become a home-movie that they can only watch close-up in the camera's viewfinder. If the baby is not asleep, they pick it up and hold it against their breasts. The men do this as confidently as the women, one of their huge calloused hands totally covering the baby's swaddled torso. Italian Madonnas are regal, their bambini adored. Here the celebration is different. The circle of illegal migrant workers sitting with their backs to the wall are marvelling at a faraway victory. Of course the baby's birth is no surprise and has been awaited. But time after time, and life being life, a victory is never assured until won. Those who haven't yet drunk take the occasion to drink, eyes a little damp. And all are equally astounded by the news of a victory from far away.

Olek, his small hand pressing against Danka's breast, drank and drank and put on weight. So did the parents. Nourishment somehow became a promise for the three of them.

One day Mirek said: You and I must go on a diet!
Why?
So you can get into your wedding dress!
She blushed for she knew it was true.
Give me three months, she said.

The vegetables are cooked and I put them through a mixer – one of those that turn by hand. I found it in the dining-room cupboard behind the soup plates. I hold the feet of the machine, which straddles a dish, firmly on to the kitchen table with my left hand, and I turn the handle with my right. It was my mother who taught me the technique when my hands were small and the practice more difficult than I imagined. Wait till you're bigger, she said.

At weddings guests are usually expansive so that they seem more numerous than they really are; the opposite happens at funerals. Nevertheless at Nowy Targ there were in reality a hundred guests.

Danka was still and calm. She looked as if she had stepped out of her bath into her dress and then into the church. She exuded freshness, a cunning freshness that had taken days to attain. Her hair was plaited with long leaves and the tiny pointed locks woven together to create a crown like a lark's nest in the grass. Everything about her when she entered the church – it would change in a few hours – was meadow.

Mirek was wearing a very light-coloured suit with a stand-up Indian-type collar and had the air of a croupier stepping out of a casino to enjoy the sunshine.

I wondered, as the pair of them walked down the aisle, how many weddings, regardless of century or place, walk past the same moment: the moment of water being drawn from a well? (The two rivers which flow through the unemployed town of Nowy Targ are called the Black Dunajca and the White.) The bride, having drawn water from the well, carries it in a pitcher on her shoulder. The bridegroom may be aware of this, but on no account should he look. The pitcher never appears in the wedding photographs because it's only visible from behind and for a five-hundredth of a second. I think we saw a pitcher sitting on Danka's shoulder for an instant.

The priest was young. The population of the town is 40,000 and it has ten priests. Unless forced by necessity, couples don't marry during Lent or Advent, nor in November since the month is said to bring matrimonial bad luck. Weddings are traditionally on Saturdays, so the celebrations can last as long as possible. The young priest officiated, I'd guess, at thirty or thirty-five weddings a year.

His voice when he spoke was intelligent. He had keen eyes, and repetition had not so far made him complacent. He knew each marriage at which he officiated had been agreed upon within an intricate web of calculation, desire, fear, bribes and love, for such is the nature of the marriage contract. Each time, however, the task he set himself was to try to locate what was pure in this web. Like a hunter going into the forest, he set out to stalk a purity, to entice it out of its cover and to let all those present, and particularly the couple involved, acknowledge it.

Not an easy task, and it wasn't necessarily simpler on the rare occasion when the woman and man were wildly in love, with scarcely any other interest, for then he risked to glimpse how desire, when mutual and passionate, is more often than not, a conspiracy of two against the cruelty of the world, apparently abandoned by God. Shreds of the purity he sought were of course always present, what made his task difficult is that a purity, when disclosed, invariably goes back into hiding. It is hard to sidle up to purity as Despina did with the wolves. Chopin succeeds in some of his mazurkas, Sappho in her few fragments of verse.

The young priest last Saturday in Nowy Targ, accomplished his task; at a certain moment he was radiant. Perhaps the purity he located, the purity which did not run for cover, resided in the ten-month-old Olek. Olek, dressed in white like his mother and father, lay awake and totally calm throughout the long ceremony in the arms of Danka's elder sister, who was sitting, smiling towards the altar, at the back of the church.

I run the water from the cold water tap over the hard-boiled eggs and I roll them between the palms of my hands so that the shells will come off easily.

The cortège moved off, the bride and groom in the first car with white pennants flying from the radio aerial and door handles. Danka, beside Mirek on the back seat, with Olek on her knees, opened the window a little to have some cool air. The drivers of the cars that followed klaxoned, impatient for music and dancing. Most of Mirek's friends had already been married for twenty years, and were familiar with the difficulties, the silences of conjugal life. Music would soon remind them of its promises.

The reception was to be held in what had previously been the canteen of the shoe factory. Some guests had proposed to walk there, for it was only a couple of kilometres away, it was sunny and there was no hurry. Amongst the walkers was a thin woman with black eyes, whose name was Jagoda, which means Berry, and she was humming a tune from her youth, ten years ago. One of her companions snapped off a branch of leaves which she waved as a wand, and accompanied Jagoda with the words of the song.

The cars came to a standstill before a barrier, which was like the red and white pole of a frontier-post. Three of the frontier guards had the marionette movements of elderly alcoholics; the other three were young men, unemployed, learning how to hassle. Hold-ups and jokes are not so different at their beginning.

Mirek got out of the car, opened the boot, where there were eighty bottles of vodka, and handed over two. One more! No question. Grins on both sides. And behind the grins, an awareness of the abyss that can claim anyone.

I scatter the cut sorrel into the soup which turns green.

Two of the musicians were playing when the newly married couple and the first guests arrived. The place was as large as a barn with a dozen tables arranged in a horseshoe at one end, and the four musicians – piano, drums, guitar and singer – at the other. Between was a dancing space the size of a threshing floor. The singer with bare shoulders and wearing trousers was as slim and short as the letter i; her voice was famous for being as wide as a horizon. Some guests as they entered glanced at her and without opening their mouths pushed forward the tips of their tongues, as if secretly testing the reed of a wind instrument whose music they hoped would accompany them all night long. Her nickname in Nowy Targ is Clarinette. She would only start singing with her voice that quivered when all the guests had arrived, not before. In the meantime she was dancing with the drummer who came from the Tatra Mountains. He was a large man and their dance gradually changed their sizes; Clarinette became as tall as a capital I, and the massive drummer became slim. This act of theirs represented the first transformation of the evening.

There was champagne to drink. There were polythene sacks like saddle bags lying on their sides with their spigot taps which, when turned forty-five degrees, let wine flow abundantly. Beer, from the village of the animals, was ordered from the waiters and served in tall steins. On each table were four open bottles of vodka and these would be replaced throughout the night whenever one was empty. Each bottle had in it a spray of dark green bison grass, which gives off a flavour a little like vervain. Mirek had been looking after the vodka for the wedding for a week.

As we talked of this and that, our eyes wandered towards Danka, not because she was making herself prominent, but because of the whiteness and extent of her dress. A rising moon. Maybe it had something to do with the silver threads of her sheath bodice. But it was also to do with her hands and pale arms as she sat there at the table. Her hands had recently learnt two sets of gestures, those of lover and those of mother. Both sets are imbued with tenderness, yet are strictly opposed. Maternal gestures reassure and calm; amorous gestures provoke and rouse. Her hands, relaxed on the tablecloth, almost looked as if just the afternoon before they had been making pastry! Her fingers though gave the game away. Danka's fingers shimmered more than the moon-silver threads, it was they who made her shine.

Children began to dance, pretending to an innocence they did not possess. Nobody who dances to music is innocent. Glancing at the children some of the middle-aged remembered how, when they were young, what was desired kept a certain distance; whereas now, even when unobtainable, the to-be-desired was too close. To change that distance – and this was the unending provocation of the music's rhythm – to change that distance, one only had to to get to one's feet and dance. Which is what some couples did.

The talk at the tables, where the eating had begun, was the talk of travellers returned home for a brief visit to the Polish Kingdom. After a vodka or two, I had the impression that the horses of a hundred riders might be tethered outside along the edge of the forest.

They were speaking about jobs, deceptions in love, cousins in Chicago, the health of Karol Wojtyła the Pope, prices, the diseases of trees, ageing, and the songs they would never forget. Whenever a topic could be turned into a game, they did so and played it.

The dishes came like good news, one after another. After each one there was an interval for drinking and dancing and measuring the improbability of so much good news. Everyone gathered there knew that news of a catastrophe comes all at once.

The Clarinette sang. Most of the songs in the world are sad. All are about stories that have finished and ended. And yet there's nothing more present and defiant than singing.

> Hair the last veil
> before everything
> a hair's breadth
> before nothing.

Hair the farewell
before light
the endlessly black
before white.

Find in me
find in me for you
my brightness.

When she stopped, the first to speak were those who
found the silence hardest to bear.

I taste the soup, add a little salt and peel the eggs. The
shells come off like brown clowns' noses.

It was time for Mirek to dance alone with Danka. Olek
was asleep in his carrycot. He would only remember the
wedding through photographs. Who knows? His parents walked alone on to the threshing floor. Everyone
watched. The satin roses on Danka's shoulder-straps
were waiting to slip from her shoulders, the roses of
her flouncing skirt were kept flying by the air-rush of
her turning. Everyone watched. The sight of the pair
of them roused many memories and often the same
question. Was what time has changed an illusion? The

music gave its own answer. The chattering voices another.

The bride was no longer meadow. Her neck rose straight from her full breast, her outstretched wings swept the floor. She was snow goose. Her whiteness grew larger. When at last they stopped dancing and, glistening with sweat, returned to their table to continue the feast, many guests were impatient for the music to start up again so they too could dance and share the music's answer, rather than that of the chattering voices.

At a certain moment I left my table and made my way across the barn. I passed the musicians, felt the rhythm of the percussion, went outside and walked between the trees on the edge of the forest. There were no horses tethered there. A man with a saxophone approached me.

Good evening, comrade, he said.

It was these words which made me recognise him. Felix Berthier.

He was a member of the brass band of the village in which I live. By trade he was a house painter who worked by himself. He addressed everybody he met as comrade – the curé, the mayor, the baker who voted fascist, the undertaker, a kid on his way to school. The greeting was offered with a smile, not mockery, as if he had lifted up the encountered one and transplanted him into another time and place where the assignation would fit.

Each month of May, on the Thursday of Ascension Day, the brass band goes to play outside the houses of one of the outlying hamlets of the village. There is a rota, so that the music comes to each hamlet once every five or six years, and the inhabitants prepare refreshments to be consumed when the concert is over. Because the trees are not yet in full leaf, the music carries a long way over the fields. The tunes played are traditional and familiar.

When a concert was finished, Felix would knock back two glasses of *gnôle*, adjust his bandsman's cap to a more jaunty angle, and wander between the barns and outhouses, or around a little chapel, playing Duke Ellington style. He proceeded slowly like a sleepwalker, and it was hard to decide whether people made way for him, or whether he found his own way along passages opened up by his playing. He seemed to be walking in that other place at that other time. This is why his eyes smiled. Undoubtedly he was, in his own way, playing for those present. The rest of the band took pains to disassociate themselves from him. The bandmaster would raise his eyes to heaven in exasperation, but occurring as it did on Ascension Day, he put up with the problem.

Felix, I asked him, can you play tonight at my friend's wedding?

Comrade, why do you think I've come? He was already stooping over his saxophone.

Fifteen years ago, on a Saturday night, Felix was playing his way home and a car knocked him over in the main street of a neighbouring village and killed him.

With the passing of the years, some of the houses he painted and the rooms he papered, needed to be redecorated, and this involved stripping down what he had done. And so it was discovered that, on many occasions, before he started papering or sticking on new panels, he scrawled messages on the walls with his large housepainter's brush: PROFIT IS SHIT. THE POOR GO TO HEAVEN. VIVE LA JUSTICE!

After midnight I heard Felix's alto-sax.

The music, like the young priest a few hours earlier, was searching for a purity. Not, of course, the same one. The music was searching for the purity of desire, of what passes between a longing and a promise: the promise of consolation that can outlast – or anyway outflank – the punishments of living.

> To shoot you
> they'll have to
> shoot thru' me.

The Clarinette's voice touched outer space, and the music attained the purity that staunches wounds.

Everyone in the barn was reminded how a life without wounds isn't worth living.

Desire is brief – a few hours or a lifetime, both are brief. Desire is brief because it occurs in defiance of the permanent. It challenges time in a fight to the death. And dancing is about that challenge.

There was only one bride there and one groom, but there were several hundred weddings; remembered, real, regretted and imaginary.

In the small hours the voice of the wedding party changed – it became younger. The older guests looked older – myself included. Some of the children were asleep on benches against the walls. Olek did not stir in his cot, fingers unfolded. The crate of empty vodka bottles grew heavier. The dishevelled musicians became the governors of the night. A waiter on his way to the kitchen took time off to dance.

Everywhere there was more white. Men had taken off their jackets and ties. Several women had kicked off their shoes and were barefoot. Mirek, in his spotless shirt and pearl-coloured suit, remained immaculate. Danka stood before the iced wedding cake, which, on its stand, was as tall as she. Then, with the same authority with which, each morning in Paris, she drew the blinds in her employers' bedroom and placed coffee on their bedside table, she cut the first portion of her own wedding cake. And as each guest ate their slice, everything that was white shone brighter.

It was at this moment that twelve men with their hands held out approached Danka and fetched Mirek. They were Gurali, sturdy men from the Tatra Mountains. Who knows, perhaps it was because of them that Danka had insisted upon being married in the unemployed town of Nowy Targ? They began to sing together; by a common accord the musicians fell silent. They sang in unison, deep chanting voices.

> Put behind the bitterness
> Now's the time to embrace.

While singing, they lifted Mirek and Danka off their feet and laid them across their arms, as though they were reclining on a shelf at shoulder height.

> Now's the time . . .

With these words and a jerk of their arms, they threw the couple high into the air. We craned our necks to watch. They were close together. Their hands could touch or reach each other's sex. Her skirt billowed in the form of a nimbostratus cloud and covered Mirek's feet. One of Mirek's hands, beyond his head, searched to turn down the sound. Imperceptibly, the two of them descended together into the waiting Gurali arms, there to be gently received, before being launched once more. They hung in the air a little longer each time.

A few hours later, at 11 a.m., the just-married and thirty wedding guests met in the main square. Most of us were licking the ice-cream cornets which are famous in Nowy Targ. Then we set off to look at a lake that is called the Eye of the Sea. Morskie Oko.

What happens is more surprising than what's invented.

In Nowy Targ during the early eighties two friends were working in the shoe factory. The family name of one of the men was Bieda, which means poor, and that of the other was Bocacz, which means rich. One day, after a trade union meeting – Solidarność was just beginning – they were picked up by a Zomo patrol. Zomo was the counter-insurgency police. They were asked their names. Bieda declared his and was smashed over the head for insolence. It was Bocacz's turn. Name? I don't have a name. So you don't have a name, eh? And he was smashed over the head for insolence. Give me your name! Bocacz. I see, so you're in this together, both of you, it's clear, said the Zomo sergeant. Poor and Rich! And they were put in a cell until they told the truth.

The walk through the forest up to the lake took three hours. Because it was summer, many people of all ages were making the same walk. When we arrived, we sat on boulders by the edge of the lake and gazed across the very still water towards the peaks. In the direction we were looking there was nothing man-made. The thousand people around us were very quiet – as if attending a performance. We munched sandwiches. Danka fed Olek. Mirek pointed to where he thought it would be possible to tickle trout. Under those rocks, he declared in his poacher's whisper. Everybody had the air of being made happy by what they had come to see. Which was what exactly? Was it the Jurassic mountain range and its reflection in the lake? Or was it the stillness of the water with its lips at the edges which never quivered?

I ask myself this as I empty the *śmietanie*, the sour cream, into a bowl in the kitchen. The sourness of *śmietanie* makes it taste less of milk and more of sex. I think we all went to Morskie Oko to look at what time does without us.

The following day, on the grassy banks of the White Dunajca, we built a fire and buried potatoes in the earth to bake them, in the same way that clay bowls, which last for centuries, are baked. The potatoes we ate hot with salt from Wieliczka and horseradish from Danka's mother's garden.

Night's falling. Something must have delayed them. I could telephone Mirek on his mobile and I don't. I prefer to wait, as this house without a doorstep does. I move into the room with the swing and the armchair.

With a little psst! the reading lamp on a table in the far corner goes out, probably the bulb, which I won't be able to replace. On the table are a pile of yellowed newspapers, some of them dating from the 1970s, a hand-compass that Mirek perhaps used when he was starting out as a forestry engineer, and a coffee tin, with nails in it. The table has a drawer and I open it with the stupid hope that I may find a light bulb, which I'll try in the lamp. There are only books, Polish novels. Underneath them, at the bottom of the drawer, is a thin pamphlet with a photograph of a woman on its cover. I naturally recognise her, her eyes with their expression of looking through an opaque wall at what lies behind it, their expression of surprised pain and sustained determination. I see the slight limp of her walk, and I hear her voice, speaking in Polish, German, Russian, the voice of the eighteen-year-old who fled Warsaw because she was going to be arrested by the Czarist police, the young voice she never lost, even when her words were like those of a venerable prophet. Rosa Luxemburg. She was first introduced to me when I was sixteen, more than twenty years after her death. She was born in nearby Zamość where Bogena goes to argue with the authorities (in vain) about her father's pension.

Who knows how the pamphlet, entitled *Centralism and Democracy*, ended up here? To add to the improbability it's in French. Yet she, her writings, her imagination were accustomed to clandestinity and clandestine travelling. They expected to be hidden in remote drawers.

The last paragraph of the pamphlet, written in 1904, argues like this: For the first time in history, the workers' movement in Russia has the chance of really becoming the instrument of the popular will. Yet look! The ego of Russian revolutionaries has made them lose their minds and talk yet again of an almighty historical leadership residing in His Highness, The Central Committee. They stand things on their heads and don't realise how the only legitimate subjectivity for any revolutionary leadership today is the ego of the working class, who want the right to make their own mistakes and to learn for themselves the dialectics of history. Let's be clear. The mistakes made by a revolutionary workers' movement are historically infinitely more precious and fecund than the infallibility of any so-called Central Committee!

Outside it is entirely dark and I hear, in the distance, the chattering of a nightjar. Seated on the swing, wearing black high lace-up shoes of thin leather, could be goatskin, with heels that are not flat – some German comrades found her choice of footwear odd – Rosa makes the swing oscillate with the regularity of a tall clock's pendulum, covering the same minimal distance of twenty centimetres back and forth, no more.

To recall and recall again the circumstances of her death. In the last days of December 1918 she and Karl

Liebknecht founded the German Communist Party. Two weeks later they were arrested in Berlin and taken to the Hotel Eden where they were interrogated, beaten up and bundled into a vehicle supposedly to be transferred to the prison of Moabit by cavalry guard officers. In reality they were taken to the Berlin Zoo and slaughtered. She had her head smashed in, and her body was thrown into the Landwehr canal.

I glance at the swing, and her abundant thick hair.

The Berlin Zoo is not far from the Botanical Gardens. From a prison cell in Wroclaw, seven months before her death, Rosa wrote to Sophie Liebknecht.

Sonitschka, your letter gave me so much joy and I reply immediately. Now you see the pleasure and comfort a visit to the Botanical Gardens can give! You should do it more often. I share your pleasure when you describe so vividly your impressions. Yes, I know those wonderful catkins of pines that are ruby-red when the trees are in flower. Those red catkins are the female flowers from which the cones are born, the cones that become so heavy they drag the branches down towards the ground. Beside them are the less obvious male flowers of a pale yellow, from which comes a golden pollen. Unfortunately, from my window here I can only see the foliage of some distant trees, can just glimpse their tops on the other side of the wall. I try to guess by the colour and the little I can see of the form, what kind of tree each one is, and I believe that, on the whole, I hardly make a mistake.

The swing is totally still now and the slatted seat hangs

at an angle to the floor, as if it had never moved or been sat upon.

Tomorrow I will do a drawing of a clematis which climbs up a pear tree behind the house. Its pears, when ripe, are reddish, and their flesh tastes slightly of juniper berries, their skins of slates in the rain.

Rosa loved birds – particularly the urban starlings who fly en masse above the streets and over the roofs. She herself was a linnet. *Hänfling* in German. A name suggesting tenderness and sharpness. I noticed the clematis a couple of hours ago, when I went out to hang a dampish eiderdown on the clothes line. Its flowers are particularly large and of a blue that verges on black, with a touch of purple. I'll do the drawing with black ink and spit and salt, which brings out the red in the ink. The drawing, if it's any good, I'll leave between the pages of the pamphlet, which I have just replaced in the drawer with the novels on top.

A beam of light illuminates the garden on the other side of the track, at first high up at the level of the tall bean-sticks, then descending to the beetroots. It extinguishes itself. The darkness is blacker. Then the beam reappears, brighter: the headlights of a car. They have arrived.

When the three of them entered the house, it immediately became larger. The roof spread its wings. Houses shrink when lived in alone, and even more so when uninhabited. Danka was carrying Olek in her arms and as she crossed the threshold from the creaking portico-hallway into the dining room, they both smiled as if their two faces were expressing a single feeling which neither could have explained.

Mirek and I began to unload the car. There were cardboard boxes, shopping bags, a folded pushchair, a cot, suitcases, a thermos box, a crate of apricots, and, last of all, the wedding dress, hanging from a hanger inside a polythene bag. Fixed to the roof of the car was a ski container, shaped like something halfway between a coffin and a kayak. It had been thrown away and left on the street in Paris and Mirek had recuperated it.

Let's take it off, said Mirek, though I'm not going to unpack it – it's full of stuff for Warsaw, nothing else.

They intended to pass a long weekend in the house without a doorstep and then drive through Lublin to Warsaw, where they would begin their new married life as planned.

Danka, with her son in her arms, walked around the house. Nothing in it seemed to surprise her. She took her time. She tried to open a window and failed. Eventually, returning to the room with the photograph of the hunter, she announced: It's big.

Olek wanted to be put down on the floor. Once there, he held on to her hands and walked a few steps, chuckling with satisfaction as if each unsteady step was a point of arrival. They saw a night butterfly. Olek stumbled and would have fallen if she hadn't been holding him. Slowly, she murmured, slowly, one step, slowly, two steps . . .

When he was sitting on the floor she caught the moth in her hands and showed it to him before putting it out of the front door. Cma! she said, Cma!

Danka had acquired another sense of time since the wedding. She could imagine looking back at the present from what, until a few days ago, was an impossibly distant future. She could imagine Olek being a father and Mirek and herself being grandparents. She was looking back at herself from a point in the future, and she was asking a question. I'm not sure to whom.

You haven't forgotten have you? You remember? It was five days after Mirek and I got married. We drove all the way from Nowy Targ and we arrived at the house I'd never seen. Mirek had talked about it as though it belonged to another life before I was born, and it was dark when we arrived, and John had prepared some soup, and Mirek was making up our big bed in the room where there was an ostrich egg in a wickerwork basket, and it was the first time for ten days that Mirek and I were going to be alone. I realised how much lay ahead, and I was happy, doubly happy, one woman stepped into my wedding dress and two stepped out – my hair was curly and auburn, remember? – and I was going to love Mirek as he deserved, I knew how much he deserved, at that time it was one of the deepest things I knew, and Olek was healthy and very strong, I was proud, one morning when

I was dressing him he accidentally gave me a biff and I had a black eye, that's how sturdy he was at ten months, I was proud, and I was walking through this house I was seeing for the very first time and I said to myself, I don't care, I don't care how long it takes and how much I have to work, and if we have to move from room to room over the years, working on room after room until the house is at last finished, it won't matter – is a house ever finished? – what I know is that I want to live here straight away and always. Remember? I can't say what made me so confident that evening, maybe you told me it would be all right, maybe that's what gave me confidence.

I'd better change him, she said out loud and picked up Olek.

I'll set the table, I said.

The table was very long, a table for committee meetings, not for meals. Two-thirds of it was encumbered with what had been casually left on leaving the house, or abruptly deposited on arrival: clothes, hand tools, a coil of rope, basins, paper bags, a cap. The end nearest the kitchen was clearer and covered with dust. I wiped it, and laid out the garlic bread, raw herring and pickled mushrooms that Mirek had brought. I fetched the ladle and steaming saucepan from the kitchen, and the eggs. Then I served the soup into bowls with the ladle, and into each bowl put two halves of an egg.

The Poles call Ken's soup *szczawiowa*. It is one of the most elementary soups in the world, and maybe that's why, as well as nourishing, it provokes dreams. For example, if you're cold it warms you and at the same time is refreshing. The acid sorrel makes the vegetables taste volatile and sharp. The eggs, which are larger than anything you usually find in a soup, have a rounded, solid taste. The sour cream, added at the last minute, permeates both. Jacob Boehme, the shoemaker who sold woollen gloves and lived a little to the west of Wroclaw in the seventeenth century, proposed that the world comes continually into existence by passing through seven phases. The first is Sourness, the second Sweetness, the third Bitterness, the fourth Warmth, and after Warmth, according to him, comes Love, to be followed by Sound and Language. I would place *zupa szczawiowa* somewhere between Warmth and Love. When you sip it, you have the impression of swallowing a place. The eggs taste of the earth of this place, the sorrel of its grass, the cream of its clouds.

We ate in silence for a moment. Danka blew on her spoon to cool it before testing whether Olek liked the soup. He did. After each spoonful he chortled and Danka wiped his mouth. Then Mirek said: You know what my dream was for a long while? It started in Paris, often when I was snarled up in the traffic, driving from one building site to another. Sometimes I thought of it when painting a ceiling. My dream was to run a little restaurant. Nothing big, twelve tables, in Zamość under the arcades, serving traditional dishes and new ones I'd introduce, using vegetables and fruit grown here in this garden, made larger for keeping chickens and rabbits too. I made up menus in the traffic jams! Crazy!

Danka put down her spoon and turned towards him with her full goose authority. If you don't try to carry out that dream now – she spoke slowly, her dark green eyes screwed up – you never will!

Mirek didn't reply. We finished the soup and chatted about other things. When nothing was said, I could hear the clock in the next room.

Olek wanted to get out of his feeding-seat and Danka took him in her arms and fed him pieces of apricot. Mirek unfastened the seat from the table and, leaving the door open, went into the room with the swing. There he attached Olek's seat to the cords, higher up than the beech-slats. He tested it, made the knots tighter and then came back to fetch the boy.

Put into the seat, Olek grasped the two cords in his tiny fists and Mirek with his huge hand gave him a gentle push. He was swinging. He went higher and higher and was more and more full of delight.

The way Danka, who had left the table to watch, the way she stood there, watching her son soar away and come back, whispered to me that within two or three months she would be pregnant again.

Each time the seat came towards him, Mirek held it for an instant in his hand, raised it a little higher, and let it go once more. The house had changed as never before in Mirek's lifetime.

I come outside to have a pee and the nightjar is singing. Kutak-kutak-kutak. Only night birds sing so long without stopping. He's much nearer than before and may be in one of the trees by the bridge. I walk down there, for I've never in my life seen a nightjar, I've only heard them. The first time I heard one was in the Epping Forest with Camellia. He eats insects all night long, she told me, and he opens his beak so wide, it's like a train tunnel! One of the toes of his foot, she went on, has a saw-edge, nobody knows why.

On each outing with Camellia in the dark or daylight I learnt names. What is this furry thing? The larva of a White Admiral. This moss? Silk wood. This knot? A clove hitch. And this? You know very well – your belly button!

There was much that could never be named. In the room of the upturned boat I told myself that the wood-grain of the varnished walls was a kind of map of the nameless, which I tried to learn by heart, in the belief that it might one day be useful. The realm of the nameless was not shapeless. I had to find my way about within it – like being in a room with solid furniture and sharp objects in pitch darkness. And anyway, most of what I knew, most of my hunches, were nameless, or their names were as long as whole books I had not yet read.

Kutak-kutak-kutak . . .

I am standing so still under the tree the nightjar is in, he starts to chatter again. And standing here under the tree, I remember a few of my hunches.

Everywhere there's pain. And, more insistent and sharper than pain, everywhere there's a waiting with expectancy.

The nightjar falls silent and another, further down the stream, replies.

Counting is a way of secretly approaching something other than what is being counted.

The Szum has the same voice as the Ching.

Liberty is not kind.

Nothing is complete, nothing is finished.

Nobody said this, yet I knew it in Gordon Avenue.

The nightjar above me flies out of the tree to join his companion and in the filtered moonlight I glimpse the white band on his tail-feathers.

Smiles invite to happiness, but they don't reveal of what kind.

Of human attributes, fragility – which is never absent – is the most precious.

I point up to the sky in the direction in which the nightjar flew. And this? I ask.

That's Andromeda, Camellia replies, I've told you many times.

I strolled back towards the house. Unless panic sets in, darkness tends to reduce hurry. There is more time. There were no lights in the windows.

I stepped up on to the concrete platform and found my

way through the creaking portico-entrance. I did not switch on the light.

The door to the bedroom was ajar. The little light coming through the window trawled like a grey net over the bed. The three of them were asleep. Olek lay against his father's chest, his hand up to his mouth and Danka was cupped around Mirek's back. A moth touched my hand in the darkness. Cma! Only the human body can be naked, and it is only humans who long and need to sleep together, skins touching all night long. Cma.

Within a week, Olek, with his determination, will learn to walk here, and Danka will ask Mirek to build a doorstep to their house.

8½

Why did you never read any of my books?

I liked books which took me to another life. That's why I read the books I did. Many. Each one was about real life, but not about what was happening to me when I found my bookmark and went on reading. When I read, I lost all sense of time. Women always wonder about other lives, most men are too ambitious to understand this. Other lives, other lives which you have lived before, or which you could have lived. And your books, I hoped, were about another life which I only wanted to imagine, not live, imagine by myself on my own, without any words. So it was better I didn't read them.

I risk to write nonsense these days.

Just write down what you find.

I'll never know what I've found.

No, you'll never know. All you have to know is whether you're lying or whether you're trying to tell the truth, you can't afford to make a mistake about that distinction any longer . . .

Acknowledgments

'We can only give what is already the other's' – Jorge Luis Borges. For this book I deeply thank: Alexandra, Andres, Anne, Arturo, Beverly, Bill, Bogena, Colum, Dan, Gareth, Geoff, Gianni, Hans, Iona, Irene, Jean, Jitka, John, Katya, Leticia, Liane, Libby, Lilo, Lisa, Lucia, Maggi, Manuel, Maria, Marisa, Michael, Mike, Nella, Paul, Pierre-Oscar, Pilar, Piotr, Ramon, Robert, Sandra, Simon, Stephan, Tonio, Victoria, Witek, Wolfram and Yves.

A NOTE ON THE AUTHOR

John Berger was born in London in 1926. His many books, innovative in form and far-reaching in their historical and political insight, include the Booker Prize-winning novel *G, To the Wedding* and *King*. Amongst his outstanding studies of art and photography are *Another Way of Telling, The Success and Failure of Picasso, Titian: Nymph and Shepherd* (with Katya Berger) and the internationally acclaimed *Ways of Seeing*. He lives and works in a small village in the French Alps, the setting for his trilogy *Into Their Labours* (*Pig Earth, Once in Europa* and *Lilac and Flag*). His collection of essays *The Shape of a Pocket* was published in 2001.

A NOTE ON THE TYPE

The text in this book is set in Granjon.
This old-style face is named after the Frenchman
Robert Granjon, a sixteenth-century letter cutter
whose italic types have often been used with the
romans of Claude Garamond. The origins of this
face, like those of Garamond, lie in the late
fifteenth-century types used by Aldus Manutius in Italy.